For my husband and sons.

~Dream big and read well~

CHAPTER ONE
DORNS AND DEATH

Walking through the final resting place of the dead makes most uneasy. While Brighton valued convenience over caution, she picked up her pace as a wind gust wanted nothing more than to usher her forward. She grimaced as icy water seeped into her sneaker. The pile of fallen leaves successfully obscured the puddle she unknowingly tromped. As she continued on the familiar path to her friend's house, twirling maple tree seeds danced before her. The thin material of her sweatshirt did little to stop the chill that now crept from head to toe. Fall was Brighton's favorite season, but this October seemed to be welcoming winter long before it was due.

As she shoved her hands deep into her pockets, the weathered clapboard house came into view, marking the halfway point. Brighton had not seen any signs of life in the home for weeks. The caretaker of the cemetery lived there until he had recently fallen ill. She focused on reaching the end of the short road that weaved its way past rows of gravestones, weathered urns, and ornate mausoleums. Huge trees lined the edge of the property, bordered by a black wrought iron fence. The cemetery spanned an entire city block, but the paved stretch was a safer alternative than walking along the overgrown path set close to the busy main road.

Just as Brighton was about to exit the cemetery, she felt her phone vibrate in her pocket.

"I'm almost at your house," she said, the glass of the phone cover cold against her cheek.

"Hey, Bright. I have some bad news. Sherry's dad is dead," Kate whispered. "And they said he recently finished reading the book."

Brighton paused as she processed what Kate was saying. It happened again. She stood motionless, but her brain was in fast-forward mode. She had many questions to ask, but no words would form. Her heart sank as she thought of how sad Sherry, their friend and classmate, must feel right now. "I'll be there in a few minutes."

After running the last quarter mile to reach the yellow bi-level, Brighton tried catching her breath as she waited for Kate to answer the door. The Honda wasn't in the drive, meaning Kate's parents were working late again.

"You know I'm here, Bright," yelled Kate.

Brighton figured as much, but even after almost six months of coming to Kate's home, she never wanted to barge in. Kate sat at the kitchen table flipping through a magazine. She fiddled with the long, chestnut brown braid draped over her shoulder. Her boldly defined almond-shaped eyes focused on the pages filled with the latest celebrity gossip.

"Are your parents working late tonight?"

"I guess. They are having a hard time keeping up with book requests," Kate answered, rolling her eyes. "You can't imagine the customers pouring in."

Kate dropped the magazine, and her glare spoke volumes while she predicted what Brighton would ask. "Listen, I don't know all of the details, but I know he wasn't sick. Also, his cousin said he recently finished reading the book."

The book. She knew the rumors surrounding the novel, and she also knew the connections made to recent deaths fueled its popularity. Brighton loved to read and appreciated a well-crafted mystery. She knew how to separate fiction from reality, but it seemed others struggled with that concept.

"I can't even imagine how Sherry and her family are feeling," Brighton said. "How can you be sure the story about the book is true? What if his cousin is saying that to make the news more interesting?"

"I know you aren't buying into the rumors, but you have to admit that if it's true, it's super weird. You didn't read *My Skull Possession* yet?"

"I haven't had time. There is just too much homework, and I haven't even started the twenty-page English research paper," Brighton answered, changing the subject.

The overstuffed cushions enveloped Brighton as she reached for the remote and settled into the familiar sofa. As she aimlessly searched for something to watch, the small aquarium gurgled as it bubbled in the corner of the room. Kate gazed at the screen without comment. The usual recap of events at Forest Creek High School and laughter over the ridiculous reality show line up didn't seem appropriate. Their end of the day wind down routine of checking out new releases on Netflix wasn't happening today. The silence broke as a car pulled up outside.

Kate leaned over the sofa, her head disappearing between the paneled drapes. "Oh, they're home now. Don't say anything about Sherry's dad. I don't feel like talking about it with them tonight. They should be able to give you a ride home, though."

Brighton was relieved she didn't need to head home through the cemetery. Kate's parents walked in the back door. Brighton heard them whispering in the kitchen.

"Oh, hi, Brighton," Kate's mother said. "Will you be staying much longer?"

"No, not tonight. I need to get going."

"Well, then, can we give you a ride home?"

"Thanks, Mrs. Dorn, that would be great," she

said while checking for new messages on her phone. Of course, there were none. She was with Kate, and her mom was at work.

"I'll see you tomorrow, Kate."

"Later, Bright," Kate said, her voice muffled as she headed to her room. Kate was the only person who never called her by her full name.

The first day Kate arrived at Forest Creek High, she sat next to Brighton in history class. Even though Kate asked her name, she called her Bright. For some reason, it was okay.

Kate had already ducked into her room, so Brighton milled around in the living room as she waited for a ride home. She studied the stack of books on the table and was surprised to see *The Supernatural Explained* resting at the top of the pile. As she picked it up to read the jacket description, Kate's mom, Joelle, tapped her on the shoulder.

"Ready to go?" Joelle asked, startling Brighton. The book fell to the floor, and Kate's dad picked it up, burying it in the far recesses of the shelf. It was not the usual Civil War history title or romance novel that served as the mainstays of their collection.

"Oh yeah. Sure." She was happy to have a ride, and just as glad Kate's parents didn't ask too many questions on the way home. Luckily, they didn't notice her exaggerated cough as she tried to disguise her sniffling.

The broken heart emoticon and pictures of her dad were too much to bear as she checked Sherry's Instagram.

As Brighton entered her home, she immediately switched on several lights. The old floorboards answered her every step with a groan as she headed to her room. Her shoulder brushed against one of the many framed pictures lining the wall of the narrow staircase. The butterscotch yellow walls and cheerful furnishings gave the illusion of newness. Although small, she felt the basic two-story served as the perfect home to share with her mom. Hours passed since lunch, but Brighton figured she would wait to eat dinner when her mom came home. She has been working many late nights at the insurance office, but the extra work meant extra money.

Just as she decided to watch a cheesy rom-com to shift focus, her mom pulled into the drive. She was happy she was home. Brighton didn't feel like being alone tonight.

"How was school? What's new?" her mother asked in her usual upbeat tone.

"School was fine. I did pretty well on my English essay."

"Oh, I knew it! I told you all of that reading would pay off!" Her mom reached over the kitchen counter and pulled her into a hug. She knew that answer would make her mom happy.

If there was one thing Laura Corley tried to instill

in Brighton from early childhood was the importance of reading. Some of her fondest memories included being curled up next to her mom and listening to her soothing voice, slightly above a whisper, reading page after page of fairy tales, scary stories, or classics. Once Brighton could learn to read on her own, she kept up the practice. Whether it was a magazine, book, or the back of a cereal box, she just needed to read. The many bookshelves placed throughout their home were a testament to this.

After helping her mom put the groceries away, she said she was headed to her room to do some homework.

"Oh, by the way, you'll have to let me know how the book is. I can't wait to check it out after you finish it. I'm dying to start it," her mom said.

She rolled her eyes, laughing sarcastically. "Great. Now you believe the hype, too. I'll be upstairs doing homework." Brighton knew her mom was unaware of the news about Sherry's dad. She was thankful she could avoid this topic tonight.

CHAPTER TWO
THE BOOK

Brighton flopped onto her bed and stared at the stars. Years ago, she placed small, plastic stickers throughout her room. They were supposed to glow in the dark, but most of the time the mint green only reflected light instead of absorbing it. Not much changed over the years as far as the decor of her small room. Ballet-slipper pink and vintage white was the dominant color scheme, and she had many shelves stacked with mysteries and thrillers that were flanked by trophies and trinkets. Some of her collection may have been too youthful for a teenager, but she felt comforted surrounded by her early childhood memories. An oversized plush llama seemed right in place among her endless bottles of moisturizers and latest beauty products that promised the clearest skin possible.

Brighton had several novels that she wanted to start and an essay to finish with a looming deadline. Instead, she reached over and grabbed the pile of books and papers stacked on her nightstand. She propped *My Skull Possession* on her knees and studied the book jacket. It was no surprise that set in the murky shadows of the midnight black cover was the universal symbol representing death, mortality, and all things poison to human nature. Brighton had come across images of skulls countless times, but this one was different. The cavernous eye sockets barely breached the top of the page, as if it was inching out of a dark recess and moving uncomfortably closer. The slackened jaw could only be imagined to communicate a guttural moan or haunting whisper. It was clear the ghastly image yearned to share an unwelcome message. *My Skull Possession* filled the lower third of the cover in faded scarlet words, directly above the author's name, Elle Rellim, in small print. There was no additional description or synopsis on the back cover. She slipped the glossy jacket away from the book and ran her finger over the same words stamped on the spine. The title page listed original copyright information and verified the story had been around for a long time. Copyright 1945 by Elle Rellim. Illustration copyright 1945 by Elle Rellim. While people said evil and darkness are captured within the pages of *My Skull Possession*, Brighton felt this was already reflected at first glance. As she flipped through the pages, she heard her mom yelling for her to come downstairs.

As she walked into the kitchen, Brighton overheard the tail end of her mom's phone conversation. She now knew about Sherry's dad. Laura Corley was not one to easily rattle, but Brighton felt it was necessary to fill her in on the missing details.

"Hon, that sounds crazy," Brighton's mom said. "Did he have any other health problems? There must have been some underlying issues. I know he was young, but let the coroner determine what happened before you go making any strange connections."

"I don't know, Mom. I'm not saying I'm buying into this, but it's a little weird how all of it went down."

Laura pulled a chair out and sat across from Brighton. She always kept herself busy and never seemed to sit down and take a break. This time she made sure nothing surrounding her served as a distraction. Her eyes were filled with compassion while trying to disguise pity.

"All I know is that ever since Kate gave you a copy of that book, she has been oddly focused on having you read it. Everything surrounding it sounds dramatic."

Her mom was almost on target with the story. After moving to Bradertown months ago, Kate's parents opened a small, independent bookstore. Brighton and Kate became close while in school, and there was something magnetic about Kate's personality. Whether it was telling stories about her days living in the South or her explanation for their math assignments, she did everything with great passion and intensity. It wasn't something Brighton was accustomed to, but she was thankful to develop a close friendship with someone she felt she could trust. Brighton could remember the day very clearly when Kate gave her a copy of *My Skull Possession*. Her enthusiasm was excessive.

"Bright, *this* is the book. Tell me you've heard of it before! I mean, there are stories of people getting scared to death after finishing it, can you imagine? I've read it, and it is terrifying, but hey, I'm still around! Take it, but don't tell my parents I gave it to you. They are sick of hearing me talk about it, as well as everyone else."

Brighton remembered Kate slipping the book into her backpack. It wasn't something she wanted to run home and read, but she didn't want to refuse it and disappoint Kate.

"Mom, I know Kate can be a little over the top, but I guess it's a little weird that Sherry's dad was in the process of finishing that book and he died. That's the third person it has happened to, and they were all kind of in the same situation, no major health issues or anything. And of course, they read the book."

Laura looked at her like she was a toddler who needed some direction. "Brighton, listen. Kate and her family own a bookstore. With the popularity of e-books and e-readers, physical stores struggle to bring in customers, especially a small mom-and-pop operation. I think it's great the Dorns are running a local business, but the truth of the matter is it's hard to stay afloat and compete. As for the intrigue surrounding *My Skull Possession*, no matter how crazy it sounds, it's driving customers to their business."

She knew her mom had a point. The buzz around this book brought in additional customer traffic into The Book Cellar. Since the significant increase in the number of people who owned a copy of the book, it wasn't far-fetched to say many, if not most people in town, had one in their house. Brighton thought about all of that. However, the Dorns weren't sensationalists. Not in the least. It was Kate who brought up how she heard two people died after reading the book. The first man who suddenly passed away also recently finished the novel. The book connection normally wouldn't be a big deal, but when asked if anything seemed out of the ordinary in the weeks leading up to his death, his wife remarked how he became somewhat of an insomniac, insistent on staying up to finish a novel. He commented on how bizarre it was, but he couldn't stop reading it. He died about a week later. The cause of death wasn't determined, but they believe it was a heart attack. None of these events would seem too remarkable or strange, until a similar thing happened about a month later, to a man about the same age. It was after this rumors and internet buzz began, mentioning the book was so frightening it could "scare" you to death.

"Well, I don't know. I'm sure it's just a bizarre co-incidence, but it is a little weird. Especially after hearing about Sherry's dad," Brighton said.

Her mom got up and resumed straightening the kitchen.

"I am sad for Sherry and her family. It's a terrible thing they are going through. But I don't think every time we read about the death of someone from our area we need to try to make a connection to a book they read. Conspiracy theories can snowball quickly. I wouldn't worry about it too much."

No matter how much Brighton tried to convince herself of a rational explanation, she knew when she talked to Kate she would interpret the events in a different light.

CHAPTER THREE
BAN THE BOOK

It was 6:10 a.m., and Brighton had a difficult time getting out of bed. She didn't get much sleep after hearing about Sherry's dad, and she felt comfortable enveloped in the warmth of the down comforter. The slight breeze from the ceiling fan combined with the heat of the radiator exaggerated the sweet scent of raspberry and vanilla throughout her room. The body spray she spilled years ago never disappeared. Her hands patted the bed searching for her phone and remote control. The blood pulsed in her temples and her hair skimmed the floor as she draped her body over the side of her bed searching for the lost items. With a swipe of her arm, a few small dust-covered plush toys rolled across the floor, in addition to her phone. Her mother would suggest filling some boxes for a yard sale for sure if she saw the additional items added to her collection. Brighton had a difficult time parting with the overflowing pile of stuffed animals and other novelties that filled the suspended toy hammock in the corner of the room.

A worn, bubblegum pink bean bag nestled between the wall and the dresser served as a comfortable place where Brighton spent many hours curled up with books, letting the plush softness surround her as she sat underneath the collection of warm and fuzzy mementos of her childhood. She tossed the smiling cupcake and pastel panda into the corner and heard the jingle of keys downstairs. Brighton knew she had to jump out of bed to catch her mom before she left. It also meant she needed to scramble to get ready in time to walk to school with Kate.

"Mom," she yelled while running into the hall. "Are you leaving now?" She didn't want to rehash their conversation from last night, but she also didn't feel like being alone.

"Yes, honey. I have to get to the office early today. Do you need a ride or are you walking to Kate's?" While her mom offered to take her, Brighton realized she already had one foot out the door and didn't want to hold her up.

"No. It's fine. I still have to get ready. I'll see you after work." As Brighton headed to her room, she heard the rapid tapping of heeled shoes against wooden steps. Her mom appeared in her doorframe.

"Hey, are you okay? I know this is a tough time, and I'm here if you want to talk," she said squeezing Brighton's shoulder. She knew her mom meant well, but she also knew she needed to get to work. Another rational explanation wouldn't do much to calm her uneasiness either.

"No, really. I'll be okay. Kate and I figure there will be a lot of kids talking about it at school today, so I'll be curious to see what they have to say. I'm sure they are just as upset for Sherry and her family.

"Oh, well, okay. You're right. It's probably best to be with your friends now, but call me if you need anything. I love you." Her mom gave her a quick hug and headed back down the stairs. As she heard her the car pull out of the drive, Brighton raced through her morning routine, so she could get out the door as soon as possible.

During her morning walk, Brighton wished she took the time to finish drying her hair or at least remembered her hooded jacket. Her wavy, wheat colored tresses felt like crisp icicles extending from her scalp. She was thankful Kate wasn't ready yet, and relished the time defrosting in the living room.

Brighton reassured her friend she looked fine after two wardrobe changes.

"Get out of here. You are the one who barely wears any makeup and still looks great," Kate said while dusting bronzer on her cheekbones.

Brighton shrugged away the backhanded compliment and glanced at her phone. "All I know is that makeup or no makeup, we better get moving."

As they reached school and rushed in, the piercing sound of the final bell greeted them. Brighton didn't have time to stop at her locker, and her ballet flats barely made a sound as she quickly scampered down the hall to her first-period class. She was still breathless as she slid into her seat and fished for her notebook in her bag. Their teacher walked in and got everyone's attention with an odd announcement.

"I am sure many of you are aware Sherry Colton's dad unexpectedly passed away last night," their English teacher, Ms. Sora, commented. "Sherry will be out of school for several days, and I will pass along as much information as I can."

While most of Brighton's classmates knew about the situation, they whispered and exchanged confused glances. Kids in her school had tragedies or other sad events occur over the years, but it was unusual for Ms. Sora to address it. There was a boy who was in a terrible accident last year and an announcement was made about a benefit held to help with medical expenses, but nothing like this.

Ms. Sora walked up and down the rows of students, studying the piles of notebooks and textbooks underneath and atop the desks.

"There is something else we need to address." After seeming satisfied following her survey of the classroom, she settled into her chair.

"I'm also certain every student is aware of rumors

circulating about a certain book that seems to be gaining attention in recent weeks. I'm not sure how many of you have the book or if you have intentions on reading it, but due to the distraction it is causing, I don't want to see it in my classroom. There are thousands of other titles you can pick for your required reading. If you have any questions, you can see me after class." She peered over her glasses and continued as if her announcement was typical for an eleventh-grade group of students. "Now, if you can take out your literature books, we are going to move on to something of true literary value. Please open to the last chapter you worked on in groups."

When the ear splitting buzz signaled class was over, everyone filed into the hall. No one stayed behind to ask questions.

CHAPTER FOUR
HAUNTED VASES, CHAIRS AND ELMO

"So, that was strange," Kate said as they left class and walked down the hall. "Can she even do that? We should be able to read what we want, right? I am tempted to have my parents try to get their hands on as many books as possible and distribute them to the entire school."

Brighton knew Kate was right. The school shouldn't try to dictate what students read. In a time when the popularity of YouTube, Netflix, and various gaming consoles surpassed regular TV, teachers should be pleased kids showed an interest in reading anything at all. However, she also understood the school's stance on the matter. It was also a distraction. The book and its related events were the main topics of conversation in recent weeks, and it was quite odd three people were now dead, with all of them recently reading the book. Or was it? The more she thought about it, the more Brighton tried to rationalize the situation. The book became so popular everyone was trying to get their hands on a copy. It was safe to say many households owned a copy of the book. So if someone died, it wouldn't be so odd if the same book was found in their house. She needed to keep reminding herself her mom's theory was probably right.

"Hello? Earth to Brighton?" Kate questioned as she waved her hands in front of Brighton. "Did you hear anything I just said? You are zoned out!"

Brighton shook her head and placed her hand above her brow. "Yeah, you're right. The school really can't tell us what to read. But I see their point."

As Brighton walked with Kate and listened to her drone on about Freedom of Speech and Freedom of the Press, she couldn't help but think she wanted to find out more info as to what really possessed the school to ban a book. Hopefully, it would make things seem a bit more logical.

Brighton told Kate she would see her at the end of the day, and she headed to the library for study hall. She had no intention of catching up on her homework. Brighton found an empty table near the back of the room. She threw her book bag down on the table, prompting some of her classmates to look up in annoyance. Brighton removed one of her notebooks and placed her phone in between the pages. Browsing the internet was frowned upon in study hall, but she knew she could disguise it. She would rather risk a reprimand for using her phone than questioned about her search history on library laptops. She decided to move to another table as the librarian shifted her focus when she saw the phone in front of her. Brighton froze after catching a glimpse of herself in the mirror behind the main desk and thought maybe she should spend more time on her morning routine. She scanned the room and realized the fluorescent lights did nothing for anyone's complexion. The heartbeat of the clock echoed in the silence as its second hand announced every advancement.

The other students were engrossed in their work, or they, too, were on their phones checking Facebook and other social media sites. Brighton took a small spiral notebook from her bag. She wanted to keep track of any info she could find. While the death of her friend's dad was too recent to uncover much information besides the obituary, it had been several weeks since Thomas Regal died as well as Jude Harner. Brighton tried searching by their names, the name of the book and other related topic terms. She came up with nothing but their actual obituaries. Her search did lead her to blogs and forums with every conspiracy theory imaginable. Of course, she wouldn't find any real news outlets saying these men died from being "scared to death." Unfortunately, the information shared on social media, blogs and forums held more weight with people than any legitimate news source. After almost one hour of fruitless searching, Brighton looked at her blank notebook. Spending time by herself with her thoughts and several search engines led her back down the path to thinking how foolish this was. A series of unfortunate events does not mean they are all related. If you find the same box of cereal in the homes of the people that died, would that mean the cereal could be the cause? As she thought about this analogy, it seemed so simple it made sense. The back and forth struggle continued as the thought lurked in the back of her mind that the three people who recently died had no prior health issues, but more importantly, they just finished reading *My Skull Possession* in recent weeks. No matter how hard Brighton tried to bargain with herself, the eerie coincidences didn't sit well with her. Just as she was about to put her phone back into her bag and take a break from her research, she noticed one highlighted result.

"*My Skull Possession* is Bradertown's Basano Vase."

She had no idea what that meant, and when she clicked on the link, it took her to a forum about ghosts and other supernatural occurrences. The story of the silver vase was only one of many that got her attention. There were accounts of household furniture being haunted, such as the Belcourt Castle chairs. Visitors said they felt chills down their spine when sitting in or near the chairs, and some claim to have been pushed down when trying to get up. She laughed as she read about an Elmo doll for a child that was programmable to say the owner's name. When the doll started to say *Kill James* the parents reached out to the toy maker. No one could figure out why the doll would be programmed to say that, and some say it was because it was possessed. As Brighton read through some of the stories, she realized how silly most sounded, but a few of the unexplainable made her think about the circumstances surrounding it.

She scrolled through the story about a haunted wooden chair that was said to be cursed by its owner. Anyone who sat in the chair previously owned by murderer Thomas Busby would suffer an unfortunate fate. It has been reported that sixty-three people who attempted to sit in the chair met untimely deaths. The chair was donated to the Thirsk Museum in the UK, where it hangs high above the ground, so no one can sit in it. Just as Brighton eagerly waited for the screen to load a picture from the museum, her connection failed. She scribbled some information in her notebook and darted out the door to walk home with Kate. She couldn't stop wondering what the connection could be between a book and a centuries-old vase.

CHAPTER FIVE
WHAT A WEDDING GIFT

"Hey Mom, do you know anything about a Basano Vase?" Kate asked while mindlessly searching through TV channels.

Brighton gave her a playful shove. She didn't think Kate would bring this topic up with anyone. Kate raised her eyebrows and shrugged her shoulders. "I think maybe Brighton is on to something," she giggled.

Brighton was not thrilled to be talking about this with anyone other than Kate. On their walk home, she mentioned what she uncovered from her research. It was the only thing Brighton was able to connect to "the book." She hoped to find out what this meant on her own. Brighton sunk into the couch, waiting to hear Mrs. Dorn's response. When Kate didn't get an answer, both she and Brighton turned around staring at Joelle Dorn who still had her back turned to them.

"Mom, I said did you ever hear about the vase we are discussing?" Kate asked with a hint of irritation in her voice.

"I heard you the first time." Kate's mom turned away from the sink and sat down at the kitchen table.

She was home earlier today while Kate's dad stayed at the store.

The house smelled of onions and garlic simmering on the stove. Brighton hoped she was making her fabulous chili, and that she would also get an invitation to stay for dinner. As Joelle sat at the table, Brighton watched as Kate's mom fiddled with her earring. She paused, still not answering Kate's question. "Why do you ask about that vase?" she finally asked.

"We were just wondering what it was, that's all. You always know all kinds of random trivia and facts like that, so I thought I'd ask." Kate's tone still seemed somewhat annoyed, especially for talking to her mother.

"No one knows if the Basano vase exists. It is alleged to be something from Italian folklore. It was a silver vase from many centuries ago."
Brighton couldn't help think this was the most enthusiasm she ever heard from Mrs. Dorn when discussing something.

"The story goes that the vase was given to a woman before her wedding. She was found dead clutching the vase. From that point on, any family member who owned the vase was said to have died from mysterious circumstances. Some say the vase itself is possessed, but not everyone believed it. Nevertheless, the family hid the vase to try to stop the alleged curse. It disappeared for years but resurfaced at an auction in 1988. The whereabouts of the vase since then are sketchy."

"That's it? What does that have to do with *My Skull Possession*? Plus, the vase is only one object. Many copies of the book are in circulation. Is someone insinuating that every copy is cursed?" Kate asked, seeming disappointed.

Brighton knew from her recent research Kate was correct. The story of possessed items is a phenomenon that has intrigued people for centuries. The allure of an object being able to harness supernatural power was both terrifying and exciting. Although Brighton never heard the story of the Basano Vase, she had heard more familiar tales of items such as dolls and furniture pieces. Brighton never put much thought into thinking any of it was true.

"Girls, while the idea of a book possessing an energy that can affect our everyday lives is a captivating notion, I sure hope you don't believe it," Joelle said. She glared at Kate, but I know her explanation addressed us both. "Your father and I run a bookstore. Somehow, we've managed to survive, but the frequency of customers flocking to an actual local store is dwindling. Even chain bookstores compete with online ordering and digital copies. When talk of this particular book created a buzz, I have to admit we did see an increase in overall sales at the store, although I'm not particularly happy about the circumstances surrounding it."

The quiet ticking of the kitchen clock served as an intermission between Kate and Joelle's spirited discussion. Brighton felt uncomfortable and guilty she was the reason this conversation started. Joelle sat back in the chair, her delicate silver bracelets sliding from her wrist as she crossed her arms in front of her.

"So, wait, you do believe that there is a connection between the book and people dying?" Kate asked her mom.

"I didn't say that. I said your father doesn't seem to mind what is driving the sales at the store, while I am not a huge fan of the idea. It doesn't mean I think the correlation is true. It means the families who lost someone shouldn't see connections to their grief splashed all over social media. The idea of a possessed book causing people to die mysteriously? I don't think so." Joelle wiped away invisible crumbs before pushing herself away from the kitchen table in haste, returning to the sink to continue cutting vegetables. The kitchen was quiet except for the clicking sound of the vegetable peeler in unison with the clock. She paused, looked up and without turning around, asked, "By the way, Brighton, have you finished the book yet?"

"I haven't even started the book. I'm not sure I'm going to read it. Not that I'm afraid, I don't have much of an interest," Brighton lied. Kate raised one eyebrow and gave her a smirk.

Joelle stood motionless at the sink, her lack of comment insinuating her surprise that Brighton was one of the people in town not interested in *My Skull Possession*.

Kate popped up off the couch and broke the awkward silence. "Come on Bright. Let's hang out in my room."

CHAPTER SIX
WHAT'S THAT SMELL?

"I know. The entire situation is weird. You should really stop by the store soon. You can't imagine the non-stop crowds of people stopping by to look for it. Some are just plain curious, but some are flat out bizarre," Kate said.

Brighton listened as Kate giggled with one of the guys from their science class on Skype. Their peers were attracted to Kate like a magnet on a regular day, but the latest notoriety surrounding her dad's store and what he was selling made Kate even more popular. Brighton sat back and studied the bedroom as Kate droned on with her conversation. While Brighton's room still tried to keep her tethered to as much of her childhood as possible, Kate's was the complete opposite. There were no boy band posters, framed inspirational quotes, stuffed animals or haphazard photo collages. Kate's bedroom wasn't as warm and fuzzy. Instead of framed pictures of friends at an amusement park, she had some beautiful shots of exotic locales she visited. A busy London street contrasted with the vibrant colors of a rainforest, but both prints were neatly framed and hanging on her wall, perfectly aligned and parallel. They flanked a recessed shelf that held only a few items on each ledge.

Brighton swung her legs off of the bed and walked over to take a closer look. Cradled in the palm of her hand, the glass skull felt like an ice cube taken straight from the freezer as it rested against her skin. Its smooth texture was interrupted by the artist's name engraved on the bottom. She carefully replaced it and picked up the clay bowl decorated with small, ceramic tiles. The light bounced off the gleaming squares, re-flecting bold colors that created a colorful kaleidoscope against the wall. Kate told her several times where each item came from, but Brighton couldn't remember if the bowl was from Cancun or Argentina. Brighton couldn't help but think that not only were the items something you would see in a display case but probably not some-thing you would see in a teenage girl's bedroom.

As she carefully replaced the souvenir, a few postcards fluttered to the floor.

"Sorry Bright, I just couldn't get him to stop yam-mering on," Kate said as she flopped down on the bed.

Brighton wasn't paying attention to what she was saying but moved in closer to get a better look at something nestled in the back of the bottom shelf.

"Kate, what is that?" she said as she pointed to the small doll leaning against a metal gargoyle bookend.

"Oh, you never noticed that? I thought I showed it to you before. That's my personal Robert the Doll. It's a replica of course. We got him in Key West. I thought for sure I told you the story before."

Kate bounded over to the shelf and reached in to bring the doll into full view. The small figure sat on a chair, dressed in a white sailor suit, clutching a little toy lion.

"The original doll is much bigger. Some say it is a mirror image of the boy who owned him. He grew up to become a prominent artist, and there were many reports of strange occurrences that happened in the doll's presence. Even years after the artist passed away, people are convinced the doll holds some supernatural power. We went to the museum in Key West, and I had to have one of the little replicas. It's just the cutest thing."

Brighton considered the purple, glittery seahorse she won at a carnival years ago cute, but she couldn't say the same for this doll. Kate smiled as she stared at it and gently placed it back on the shelf. She had an eclectic collection of souvenirs from her trips, but Brighton didn't know the backstory behind all of them, especially Robert the Doll.

Brighton looked at the scenic postcards scattered by her feet. "I'm sorry. I knocked these off of the shelf," she said, shuffling through the pictures. "Are these mementos or from friends?" As she flipped the card over to read about the sprawling mansion featured on the front, Kate snatched it from her hands.

"Where were they? I didn't think I still had those. They are just some neat postcards I collected," she said. Kate hurriedly tucked them in a book and placed it at the back of the shelf.

"I'm hungry. Do you want to get a snack before you head home? Better yet, can you stay for some chili?" Kate asked, changing the subject.

"I'm good. I'm probably going to head out soon. My mom is going to be home early tonight." Normally she would have wanted to stay for dinner, but she had her fill of discussions of possessed objects and haunted stories.

The granite countertops gleamed with no visible clutter to be found anywhere in the kitchen. The only sound was the bubbling of the chili simmering on the stove. A dim light above the range cast a soft glow in the corner of the kitchen. Joelle appeared just as Brighton reached the door.

"I have no idea what time Mr. Dorn will be home. I can take you home now unless you changed your mind about dinner."

"That's okay, Mrs. Dorn. I told Kate that I wanted to get home early to have dinner with my mom. I don't mind walking while it's still light out."

"Okay, if you insist. Be careful walking home," Joelle said as Brighton headed for the door. Just as her hand reached for the doorknob, Brighton felt a slight grasp on her shoulder.

"Are you sure you don't want to stay for dinner? Kate does enjoy having you over," Joelle asked.

"Thanks for the offer, but I should get going. I'm sure I'll see you tomorrow."

Brighton slowly started walking home. Her mind swirled with thoughts of creepy dolls and haunted vases. At this time of day, her usual pace was lightning speed through the cemetery, and her focus transfixed on the gate leading her to an exit. She slowed her stride and watched the wavering pumpkin orange and lemon-yellow beams filter through the remaining leaves of the towering maple trees. As she walked farther, she saw the rays bouncing off the stained glass windows of the small mausoleum situated to the right. Brighton laughed when she thought of the word mausoleum and the conversation from the other day. When she and Kate walked through here previously, Kate corrected her when she erroneously referred to them as crypts. It turns out the technical name for it is vestibule mausoleum, with family crypts stacked inside. Brighton had to admit since Kate moved to town with her parents, she had deep conversations that were more colorful than any of the boring gossip of normal teenage life at their school.

The square granite mausoleum was flanked by a column on each side of the structure. The weathered stone steps were interrupted by drab weeds yearning to break free from the cracks in the middle of each slab. Someone did maintain this cemetery, but its upkeep was minimal and usually sustained closer to the holidays.

The small building had ornate stained glass windows on opposing walls and an entry that was slightly ajar. Although the door was open, there was a massive black iron gate securely locked. The remaining sunlight cast a warm glow surrounding the mausoleum. The metal felt like an ice shard against Brighton's forehead as she leaned forward and peered through the black gate to get a closer look. She jumped as it shifted ever so slightly, but the lock prevented any additional movement. She couldn't make out the names and dates inscribed but knew from the aging surroundings it wasn't recent. The leaves that had blown in through the open gate rustled behind her, and the light started to fade. Sunset was coming, and trepidation replaced her curiosity. That's when she heard it.

"Brighton," someone whispered. She winced as her shoulder hit the gate when she jumped forward. She didn't see anyone else when she entered the cemetery, let alone someone that knew her. Had it come from the mausoleum? She knew how ridiculous that was, and knew she must have been hearing things. Everything she was reading and thinking about was finally getting to her. Her heart raced, and her blood pounded in her ears. She needed to calm down, but that's when she heard it again.

There was no mistake that it was her name. She leaned forward, fingers clenching the gate before her. Since the sun was setting, it now made it more difficult to see inside. Her ears and eyes strained to find the source of the chilling sound echoing in front of her.

"Briiiiighton." the whisper echoed, followed by giggling. "Behind you, silly, it's me."

As she turned around after hearing the familiar voice, she saw Kate, crouched down, partially obscured by a tree. Her hair tumbled out of her pink hoodie as she fell forward and steadied herself with one hand on the ground.

"I couldn't help it. I ran after you because my mom said it seemed like something was wrong when you left. I wanted to make sure everything was okay. That's when I saw you leaning against this." Kate walked over and tapped on the marble column at the entrance to the mausoleum. "I know you usually zip through here, so I was surprised to see you stopped on the side of the road. This place is creepy but in a neat kind of way. I'll admit I find myself just wandering around checking things out, too."

Kate walked over to the same place Brighton was standing and pressed her face against the gated doorway. Pretty Kate with her long brown hair cascading down her back, her thin, graceful fingers reaching through the bars, her pink lacquered nails shining in the very little remaining light that surrounded them. Flakes of rust and black paint fluttered down around her. She turned and smiled her perfect lip-glossed grin at Brighton. She was a sharp contrast against the backdrop.

"I'm sorry, Bright. I didn't mean to scare you. I couldn't help calling your name while you seemed so involved in what you were doing. Since that door is open, the sound echoes off the back of the wall. It makes it seem like it is coming from inside."

Brighton felt foolish, only to realize someone was playing a joke on her.

"Yeah, I'm fully aware of that now, Kate. Thanks a lot."

"Oh, I'm sorry. I didn't mean to get you flustered." She walked over to Brighton and outstretched her arms. "Hugs?" she said with an apologetic look on her face.

Brighton gave her a quick hug, so she could leave and get out of the cemetery before darkness fully set in. The smell of vanilla with a hint of warm cinnamon wafted around Kate.

"Did you notice the smell?" Kate asked.

Brighton wondered if Kate read her mind. She was about to say she did notice the strong cupcake scent, but Kate didn't give her a chance.

"Before we leave, just come over here. Can you smell it?" Kate once again peered into the mausoleum. She inhaled deeply. Her lashes seemed even longer when she closed her eyes. Her eyelids sparkled like a cotton candy sunset.

"You can't mistake it. It's like ripe fruit, but musky at the same time, if that makes sense."

Brighton gave Kate a quizzical look and started to walk away. "You're weird. I don't notice the scent of ripe fruit, but I *do* notice that someone used too much vanilla lotion and body spray. Come on. I need to get home."

"Very funny, Bright! No, really, stand here and tell me you don't smell that."

Brighton knew Kate would not give up until she gave in. She stood by the door and made an exaggerated sniffing sound. "I guess it smells like musty leaves and dirt."

Kate gazed forward. "I don't know, I can't place it, but maybe you're right. It's the combination of mustiness, leaves and dirt." When she realized Brighton wasn't answering her, she continued. "I do notice it at every single mausoleum here. Do you think maybe that is what death smells like?" Kate said, her expression as serious as a funeral itself.

Brighton grabbed her arm and walked her back to the road. "Oh my God, please already. You're weird. I still say your overuse of fragrance is the only thing overpowering here. Let's go home."

Kate laughed as Brighton talked about how silly

she felt by thinking someone was talking to her from the mausoleum. She didn't want Kate to think their conversation unnerved her. She felt that poking fun at her own expense was the best way to change the subject.

Brighton figured she would head back to Kate's house with her and take her mom's offer of a ride home after all. The absence of the sunlight plunged the path ahead of them into abrupt darkness. Leaves drew circles around their feet as the wind felt like an icy hand ushering them toward the gate. Brighton was relieved they were getting out of the cemetery and leaving behind the awkward conversation about mausoleums and the smell of death.

"I'm sure my mom will be happy to give you a ride home," Kate said. Brighton knew she would, and figured that would be a better option than walking home the long way, and definitely better than through the darkness of the cemetery that lost its golden gleam from less than an hour ago.

Chapter Seven
The Book Cellar

As Brighton arrived at her house, she was relieved to see her mom's car parked out front.

"Hey Mom, you're home," she said as she leaned over and gave her a quick kiss on the cheek.

"Well, hi there. You seem to be in a good mood. How was school? Anything going on over at the Dorn's house today?"

"Not much." Brighton didn't feel like telling her mom how it disturbed her that Kate followed her into the cemetery with the intent of surprising her, not to mention the bizarre conversation that ensued about family strolls through the graveyard and the smell of death. Brighton thought that a solid night's rest, with her phone and computer off, would make everything seem less intense in the morning. First, she needed to do something.

"Mom, I have a favor to ask. Can you give me a ride somewhere? I promise it won't take long."

"Sure. We can eat dinner when we get back," Laura said while grabbing her keys.

"Where are we going?"

"I want to swing by The Book Cellar. There's something there I want to find."

Brighton did want to stop by the Dorn's bookshop, but it wasn't something she wanted to find—it was someone. Kate offered limitless information when it came to stories surrounding *My Skull Possession*, but Brighton knew little about the man responsible for the town's obsession with a book.

As they headed over to the bookstore, the glass felt cool as Brighton leaned her head against the window of her mom's car. The dim, interior lighting cast a tranquil glow around them. She didn't mind the uninterrupted classical music station taking the place of conversation. An old candle-shaped air freshener lodged between the seats for months still gently released the faint scent of sage and citrus. The peaceful travel balanced the chaos of the day.

Brighton stared at the tangled debris that lay parallel to their route. It seemed to take years to complete the concrete bridge project, and everyone watched the demolition of the old structure. Twisted metal posts stuck out of the rushing, dark water, like desperate arms reaching for help. When the river was low, it was an eyesore like much of the town. Some of the restaurants and stores that popped up in recent years were still going strong. Those that didn't make it created uninhabited barren spaces speckled throughout their community.

The darkened windows with few traces of previous activity did not do much to add to the attractiveness of the downtown, especially in bringing new tenants.

The Book Cellar somehow managed to do well enough to stay open. Brighton had to admit she was shocked someone opened an independently-owned bookstore. Even though the store wasn't around for a year yet, she was happy to see it survive. She loved supporting local business any time she could.

As her mom slowed the car, Brighton reassured they would find parking in front of the store. The moss green building served as a stark contrast against the other vacant, dilapidated spaces. Light spilled onto the sidewalk from the vast wooden framed windows, attracting customers to the ornate door nestled between. Brighton pushed the distressed brass door handle and let her mother enter first.

"I know I said it before, but I sure do like the feel of this place," Laura said as she paused to look at the expanse of books and shelves in front of them.

"It does have a cozy feel," Brighton said as she absentmindedly looked at some of the titles stacked around them. Other local book stores she had visited didn't share the same intimacy. They also seemed to follow the same model of dusty shelves crammed haphazardly with tons of books. That was not the case at The Book Cellar. The walls were lined from floor to ceiling with wooden shelves. The cases weren't painted but instead washed with a green stain, to allow the grain to show through. The floors seemed to be original to the building, and the sanded, worn finish was topped with a very slight sheen. Glass tulip-shaped lights were suspended by a brass chain evenly spaced across the ceiling, with a warm yellow hue beckoning customers to enter the store. Rather than a musty smell, the area had the strong scent of furniture polish and the fragrant aroma of freshly ground coffee beans. While the store did not have a cafe or coffee bar, the Dorns always had coffee brewing.

The checkout counter blended in with the rest of the store, flanked by bookshelves and surrounded by glass cabinets. Mr. Dorn was staring at the register and examining a little slip of paper. He was here working late, just like Kate always said.

"Oh, hi. I'm sorry. I didn't even see you standing there. I need to get a bell on the door," Pat Dorn said. As he looked up from what he was doing, he realized who waited for him to finish. "Brighton, it's you. Mrs. Corley, what a pleasant surprise." Mr. Dorn seemed flustered as he replaced the stacks of bills into the drawer. He thumbed through several checks and traced his finger down the length of the green ledger book. The keys clanged against the register as he shoved one of them into the lock. As he placed them into his pocket, he swooped down with his other arm, collecting a mess of papers and folders. "Just trying to keep things balanced and keep pace with the crazy inventory issues," he said with a sigh of relief.

Brighton glanced at her mother and around the empty store. Inventory issues didn't seem to be a problem with all of the well-stocked shelves. Who was she to judge? She never ran a store before.

"But tell me, what can I help you ladies with tonight?" he asked. His weak smile wasn't genuine, and Brighton could tell he was ready to go home. He fidgeted with his collar on his shirt and straightened it, so it rested neatly under his burgundy wool sweater. Brighton studied his face, and couldn't see much resemblance in Kate, except for the eyes. They both had a unique whiskey brown color, which at times reflected hints of copper, making them almost sparkle. His nose was narrow, but it fit the elongated shape of his face. His curly hair was a reddish brown, the hairline slightly receding.

"Well, my mom and I were in town, and we thought we would drop in," she said as she gave her mother a nervous smile. We were hoping you had a copy of *My Skull Possession* on hand. One of her friends was looking for it."

Laura Corley's eyes opened wide, and she pursed her lips. Thankfully she agreed to play along. Brighton knew she would have to explain this on the way home.

"Yeah, everyone is talking about this book. I didn't want to take Brighton's copy of it, so I thought I would buy my own. For a friend," she lied. Brighton hoped he didn't see through it.

"Well, I'm sorry to say, but they are totally out of stock right now. Keeping the books on the shelves is hard. I do expect a shipment tomorrow. The delivery was due tonight, but it looks like our courier guy isn't going to show up."

"Courier guy? I don't know much about the business. How do books get delivered?" Laura asked.

"We usually order all of our books through a catalog from a specific bookseller. They take books back that we don't sell, and we can get a refund on them. From time to time, we get approached by self-published authors to carry their books. Most of the time we have to decline, for obvious reasons. They can't give us the discount that larger booksellers would, plus, they rarely want to take inventory back. That is not the case with this book, that's for sure."

"So the author of this book is self-published? Is he the courier delivering them?" Brighton asked. "I thought the book was old. Doesn't the imprint say it was written in the 1940s? How is that being self-published now?"

Mr. Dorn didn't continue his story but instead walked to the front of the store to flip the sign to show they were closed. The sharp click of a deadbolt followed by the dimming of the overhead lights made Brighton slightly uneasy. She looked at her mom who seemed more annoyed to be here so late, since Brighton whisked her out of the house the minute she got home. The glass checkout counter was small, and that is when Brighton noticed some objects in the glass case below. There was no theme, and no for sale stickers posted. The display contained similar items found in Kate's room. As she bent down to look at a crystal skull gleaming from the second shelf, she noticed Mr. Dorn's shoes in front of her.

"Sorry. I wanted to close up in case any last-minute shoppers wandered in," he said. He motioned to the front of the door as if he was waiting for someone to walk in.

"Look, Mr. Dorn, we're sure you want to get home. We've taken enough of your time. Brighton and I can stop back another time," Laura said. As she was fishing in her purse for her keys, Mr. Dorn interrupted.

"Oh, I don't mind. You can't imagine how many questions I get about this book daily. If I am here myself, it's sometimes hard to talk at great length when you are multi-tasking. I find the situation interesting, as a matter of fact," Mr. Dorn said.

As the story progressed, Brighton became more confused. "So back to the imprint and publication date. Why does it say 1945?"

"The original story was published in 1945. Due to several clauses in the Copyright Act, the rights reverted to the author who passed away. The family of the author then had the rights, and this person claims to be one of the only distant relatives of the author. They found the story worthy of being published but had a hard time finding representation by a literary agent or getting published from any publishing house. Again, I usually don't accept self-published authors, but this person was very persistent, and the story behind it was very compelling. Plus, I couldn't resist something written by a local author."

Mr. Dorn did have a lot of information, but it still left Brighton with unanswered questions.

"That background is very interesting, but you are leaving out the most important part. What made it so popular? Is it that frightening of a book that it is scaring people to death? What does the author, or agent, publisher, whatever they are, what do they have to say about that?" Brighton asked. She was finally able to ask about everything she had been wondering.

"Come on, Brighton. Really? I told you that was just a coincidence, and now you are playing into this as much as everyone else on social media," her mom said. "Mr. Dorn, I'm sorry. I'm sure you hear this all day. We will leave you to close up so you can get home," she said while guiding Brighton toward the door. "If you could just let us out."

Instead of letting them out of the store, Mr. Dorn strode over to one of the bookshelves and grabbed an ordinary black book, placing it on the counter in front of them. "This is it. This is what all of the hype is about, and this is what is bringing in customers from all over to get their hands on a copy."

Brighton picked up the book and looked at the small gray imprint centered on the plain black cover. It was a tiny skull, approximately one-quarter of the way down.

"That's not it," she said. "*My Skull Possession* has a different cover. I wouldn't forget the picture in a million years. This isn't it." She put it back onto the counter. Although small, the book made a thud that echoed through the store. Mr. Dorn didn't lift his head but smirked as he reached over to replace the book with its spine exposed.

"Actually, yes, it is, Brighton," he said with a twinge of annoyance in his voice. On the spine of the book were the title and author she had seen before.

"What you are thinking of is the jacket cover that is on all of the reprint copies. This edition is the original that I received for review. It's the same thing," he said while handing the copy to Brighton.

She slowly flipped through the pages but had nothing to compare it to since she never read the book.

"As for the rumors you have been hearing, I'm

not sure if it is an internet sensation that got blown out of proportion, but as your mother said, I, too, believe it has more to do with coincidence than anything," Mr. Dorn said while giving Laura a playful smile.

"Have you heard of people saying that it is possessed?" Brighton asked.

"That's it, we're going," Laura said. "Thanks again, Mr. Dorn. If you could show us out."

Mr. Dorn grabbed a few folders and shut off the lights in the glass case. "It's fine. I'll follow you out. Brighton, it sounds like you have been talking to my daughter about this. I understand circumstances are leading many to believe there is some romantic notion that this book is somewhat powerful in many senses of the word. Let me give you my take on the situation. Someone is taking advantage of a long-lost relative's work, and when the right opportunities aligned, they ran with it. If you make something unattainable or unexplained, people want it. When you add in a little drama by possibly making it a little dangerous, you can create a frenzy with people wanting to get their hands on a copy. Do I think the story will scare you to death? No. No storyline can do that. Do I think it is cursed? I highly doubt it. Is it selling many more copies than I ever imagined? Yes, and with that being said, I will continue to buy cases of this book from our unconventional bookseller."

Brighton shoved her hands in her pockets, staring down at the sidewalk as she and her mom waited for Mr. Dorn to lock the door.

"Oh, Mr. Dorn. There is one more thing. Did you have as much luck selling the book before you moved here?" Brighton asked. She knew she may have pushed her luck with the last question.

Pat Dorn tilted his head as he tried the door to confirm it was locked. Brighton couldn't tell if the weary look on his face lent itself to annoyance or just being plain old tired.

"We didn't have the book to sell before we moved here." He offered no additional insight into *My Skull Possession*. "Good night, ladies. I hope my explanation made some sense. Laura, I'm sorry I don't have another copy right now."

"Another copy?" Laura said as she turned to face Mr. Dorn.

"Wasn't that the reason you came here? For a copy of the book?" he asked playfully.

Brighton was happy the lights from the store no longer illuminated the front of the building. The nearest street light was two buildings down, and a few cars were driving in the vicinity. She was thankful he couldn't see her face turn bright red with embarrassment. She tried not to make eye contact, guarding the secret to the real reason why they came to the bookstore. She hoped to find out why, and if, Mr. Dorn was at the store so late every night. She also hoped to find out more information about the book. Brighton was fairly satisfied on both fronts.

She buried her head, intently staring at her phone on the ride home. She mindlessly scrolled through Facebook, hoping her mother would not feel like talking, but knowing very well that she would.

"You, know, Brighton, I thought you were pretty rude at Mr. Dorn's shop," she said without taking her eyes off the road. "Your rapid fire questions were kind of embarrassing."

Brighton could tell her mother was annoyed. For the most part, Laura Corley always had a positive attitude. Brighton looked over at her mom, her gaze fixated on the road. There was no positive reinforcement, no discussion of the day, no comments on how quaint the bookstore was. Yes, Brighton's mom was annoyed. She strummed her fingers on the steering wheel and noticed Brighton staring at her.

"What?" she asked while darting her eyes from Brighton to the road.

"Nothing, it's fine. I'm just tired tonight. I probably shouldn't have asked you to take me out tonight. I'm sorry."

Brighton was pleased to find Mr. Dorn working late. Kate always talked about how her dad was rarely around, and when he was, he wasn't in the mood to discuss anything. The information Mr. Dorn shared with Brighton about *My Skull Possession* consisted of details she was already familiar with. She wished he elaborated on how he lucked out by not only having such success with launching the new store but even greater success with one of the most sought after books in the area. Brighton thought about how The Book Cellar didn't seem swamped, but maybe it was because they showed up near closing time.

She looked at her mom again, disappointed to see the slight grimace remained on her face. No matter the situation, she usually had a smile or at least a calm, content look. That was not the case tonight.

"Well, let's not give people such a hard time going forward, okay?" she said, shifting back to her positive self. "Mr. Dorn seems like a nice man, and I feel like you gave him quite the opposition back there."

Brighton nodded, knowing her acknowledgment probably went unnoticed in the dark car. Her stomach rumbled reminding her they also postponed dinner to accommodate her last-minute request.

"What are we having for dinner? Leftovers are fine with me. The roast beef you made yesterday was good. I can eat that again," she said. Brighton tried to shift the conversation, but she knew it would take more than cooking compliments.

CHAPTER EIGHT
POWER OF PERSUASION

As soon as they finished dinner, Brighton headed to her room. She rummaged through her backpack and pulled out the book she brought home from school. Brighton reclined onto her bed, positioning several throw pillows behind her. While she usually didn't believe stories such as "The Basano Vase", she was intrigued. As she flipped through the pages, many of the items mentioned involved dolls, statues, and paintings. The story of the Basano Vase also had an entire chapter dedicated to it in the book. Haunted chairs, wedding dresses, and storage boxes were all connected to unexplained events that led to the timely demise of those who purchased these objects in question. As Brighton read these stories, she agreed they were creepy, but many of the stories also ended with explanations for the supposed supernatural phenomenon. Experts debunked most of the legends, demonstrating how and why items were considered to be cursed, but then were able to prove otherwise. This applied to most of the situations. As for the others, there was no other explanation for these mysterious occurrences. Some were famous for bringing bad luck, and several movies were made about the surrounding events. Just as Brighton was about to turn the TV on and try to get her mind onto something else, she stopped at one of the last chapters.

> Haunted or cursed books always surface as something that can be inhabited by a demonic spirit or entity. While some think a curse or spell was cast on some of the books in question, usually it is something more logical than that. The power of persuasion is a driving force. If enough people talk about strange occurrences they noticed while having a book or any item for that matter, then others may think they are experiencing the same thing. Take for example the idea that pets seem to act strangely once their owner starts reading the book. It is possible that someone becomes engrossed in the book, ignoring their pet in return. A dog may act strangely looking for attention. Others hear strange sounds or get the feeling that someone is watching them. As soon as they tell someone what they experienced, you can bet that when lending a book to a friend, they will be thinking twice about every creak and groan they hear. They fail

to mention that the same creaks and groans were probably experienced when they read trashy romance just weeks before. The power of persuasion is the element that can sometimes be most terrifying.

"The power of persuasion is the element that can sometimes be most terrifying," Brighton said out loud. She needed to hear herself say it. It made sense. The more sensationalized the book became the more people would want to get their hands on a copy. People love to be scared, and most of them probably didn't think anything bad could happen to them. If there was the very slight remote chance that they may have a less than desirable experience, isn't that risk thrilling? If everyone else thought the book seemed scary and made their adrenaline pump, shouldn't I be experiencing the same thing? "Persuasion," she muttered again.

"Did you say something, hon?" her mom said while poking her head into her bedroom.

"I'm sorry, what?"

"I thought I heard you talking to someone."

"No, I was reading something out loud, trying to make sense of it. I'm going to bed soon, just going to watch some TV first," Brighton said while picking up the remote.

She kicked the book off of the bottom of the bed,

so her mother wouldn't see the title. She didn't want to entertain questions about her choice of books, or why she was talking to herself. Brighton was disturbed by some of the creepy encounters she just read about, but she was also somewhat relieved persuasion probably played a more prominent role. She found a cooking show where the final contestants had to prepare a full meal from the ingredients provided. As she watched the chefs struggling to pair the bizarre food on the table in front of them, she didn't even flinch when she fell asleep and knocked the remote on to the floor.

Brighton sat up and gasped. She was sweating, and her heart hammered in her chest. Brighton couldn't remember her dream, but she did recall feeling like she was running from something. Fitful shadows danced against the wall as the blinds thrashed against an open window. Cold, billowing air and interrupted moonlight poured into her room. She didn't mind the icy blast. Brighton tripped on something as she got up to grab the bottle of water on her desk. She picked up the book and instantly remembered what caused her such distress before she fell asleep. The visit to the bookstore, walk through the cemetery, and late night reading of all things eerie was sure to be the culprit of bad dreams. She felt around her bed for her phone but couldn't seem to find it. Her hand slid across the nightstand, and the sticky feel reminded her that she shouldn't leave cups and dishes on her furniture. As she was about to give up looking for her phone, she reached her hand between the bed and the wall. She felt the rubber case protecting her phone, pulled it out and tossed it on her comforter. Hoping to still get a few hours of sleep before waking up for school, Brighton refrained from turning on the lights. After 10 p.m., her phone was set to dim automatically. There was no denying what illuminated the small screen as she checked for calls and messages. Eight missed calls. Two new messages. Brighton knew she wasn't going back to sleep now.

KATE: "Brighton, please answer my calls. I need to talk to you, ASAP."

KATE: "You must be sleeping. I'll talk to you tomorrow. It happened again. Someone just bought a book from my dad's store last night. On the way home from The Book Cellar, they got into an accident. They died, Brighton."

Chapter Nine
The Accident

Brighton tossed and turned until 5:30 a.m. and gave up on falling back to sleep. She padded her way downstairs to make breakfast, fumbling for the remote to catch local news updates sure to have headlines of an accident. As the news anchor discussed some issues the school board was having, and then cutting to the weather with an un-eventful forecast, Brighton was surprised there was no mention of a car accident. She filled the coffee pot with water and opened a new bag of dark roast grind. The pungent smell gave a jolt to her senses, and Brighton eagerly waited to hear the gurgling sound. She liked her coffee black, but she set out the sugar and hazelnut creamer for her mom, who preferred it a little sweeter. Still no mention of an accident. As Brighton placed an English muffin in the toaster, her mother yawned while turning on the lights in the kitchen.

"No lights on? You are like a mole scurrying around the kitchen. Ah, but you already made coffee and brought the paper in. Perfect." Laura shuffled across the kitchen, rummaging in the cabinet for her favorite mug. "It looks like you were doing some heavy reading last night. I turned your TV and lamp off. You seemed wiped out. I didn't even bother waking you up to get changed. Didn't see your phone, but figured you had your alarm set."

Brighton grabbed her cup of coffee and watched as the butter melted into small rivers flowing into the crevices of the muffin. As she made small talk with her mom, avoiding any conversation about the messages she received just a few hours ago, the news anchor cut in with another local news update.

"Breaking news overnight. A violent one vehicle accident proved fatal for a local man. A car traveling late last night on Bramble Road in Forest Creek Township left the roadway, causing the vehicle to strike several trees. The man's name has not been released pending an investigation and notification to next of kin."

Luckily, the cup was empty and it didn't smash as Brighton knocked it off the counter.

"Ugh, sorry about that, it didn't break," she said, holding it up before placing it in the sink.

Her mother glanced over for a second and continued to scan the newspaper. As Brighton's foot touched the first step, her mother called out to her.

"Hey hon, before you go upstairs, I wanted to ask you something."

She slowly turned back down the steps and prepared herself for the conversation.

"Yeah mom?" she said, her grip tight on the back of the chair.

"Oh, I just wanted to let you know that the weather is bad, so I can drop you off at school. Do you want a ride?"

The rivulets of rain cascaded down the windshield. Brighton leaned her temple against the window, watching everything pass by in a dreary, wet blur. Her stomach was queasy, and her head felt as if it was stuck in a vice. Inhale. Hold breath. Exhale. The calming technique didn't work, and each expelled breath made her feel worse.

Typically, on a day when the weather would cooperate, she would hop out the door and head to school, but today the torrents of rain and strong wind stopped her from immediately leaving the house. Brighton had no choice today. Her hand trembled as she shoved notebooks into her book bag.

"Are you okay?" Laura asked.

"I'm fine."

Her mom gave her a quizzical look and continued to focus on the road. The rain was coming down harder now, and it made it almost impossible to see. Although the weather was not helping to bolster Brighton's mood, she was thankful that it served as a distraction by preventing her mom from asking her too many questions.

The story about the accident didn't seem to affect her. It did quite the opposite for Brighton.

The car slowed as they approached the school. They sat in line behind other students who were also waiting to be dropped off. The sound of music or even talk radio would be most appreciated to fill the silent void. The squeaking of breaks, slamming of doors and the constant quick whir from the fast-moving wipers was the only background noise. The tail lights from the car in front of them sprayed a pattern of crimson onto the water droplets on the windshield. Mindlessly, Brighton concentrated on the blood red dots in front of her. She clutched the strap from her book bag so tightly that her nails made small crescent indentations in her palms. As the car was nearly parallel with the entrance to the school, she quickly grabbed the door handle.

"Hey, don't I get a goodbye?" Laura asked. She leaned over to the passenger side, resting her hand on the seat. Her face squinted, and her regularly cheerful expression replaced with a frown that reflected worry and concern.

Most of the time Brighton and her mom were on the same page. While some of her friends complained about their parents, Brighton and her mom got along very well. She didn't expect her mother to understand the gravity of the situation. Only Kate would get it. She needed to see Kate.

"Bye, Mom. See you later, love you," she said as she ducked her head back into the car, gave a forced smile and quickly retreated, slamming the door. She hoped that would suffice to ease her mother's concerns for the time being. She didn't know who or what could ease her worries. She tossed her book bag over her shoulder and darted through the ankle-deep puddles on the sidewalk in front of her. Her umbrella remained tucked in the mesh compartment in her bag. It was useless to try to take cover from the wind which was driving sheets of rain almost horizontally.

As she entered the school, the fluorescent lights nearly blinded her vision. It was in stark contrast to the dark start of her day. Her sneakers were soaked, and she could feel her damp curls springing up by the second. The re-energized scent of honeysuckle, tempered with the slightest touch of vanilla gently wafted around her. She dropped her bag on the floor, and quickly wound her hair in the tie she always had on her wrist. Students scurried throughout the hall in front of her. She wondered if they were oblivious to what happened. Lockers slammed while wet sneakers annoyingly screeched against the tile floor.

As she made her way to her locker, the comforting floral and warm scent was replaced by the mix of institutional floor cleaner, burnt toast from the cafeteria, and wet kids. She opened her locker, and slid out of her damp jacket, carefully hanging it on the small metal hook. She gasped as something slammed into her locker.

"Hey! Didn't you hear me yelling at you from down the hall? I was waving my arms trying to get your attention."

"I'm sorry. I rushed to the school to get out of the rain. I guess I didn't hear you."

"Umm, you didn't. I mean rush in that is. You looked like a zombie standing at the entrance. I know it's a miserable start of the day, but snap out of it," Kate said.

As Brighton grabbed one of her books from the top of her locker, she glared at Kate.

"I may not be chipper like you this morning, but aren't you concerned about what happened last night? I think it's bizarre. I'm sure no one else is talking about it, but they would be if they knew all of the details."

Kate lowered her voice. "Maybe we should talk about it later, okay? My dad said not to make a big deal about it."

Brighton wondered what happened to Kate's sense of urgency expressed in texts last night.

"You were the one who kept texting me last night. And wait, didn't the accident happen last night? How did you know that they just bought the book from your dad? I was at the store last night, and no one bought a book when I was there."

Kate hugged her books and looked down at the floor, thinking before she responded to Brighton.

Brighton didn't mean for that bit of information to come out. She didn't want to explain why she was at The Book Cellar yesterday.

"You were at the store last night? For what?" she asked.

Brighton wasn't sure why she was so defensive, but she did know she needed to get to class. "Never mind. We'll talk later." She grabbed her notebooks and stepped away from Kate.

"Sure, whatever. I'll talk to you later." With that, Kate adjusted her purse on her shoulder and headed down the hall. Hopefully, Brighton would make sense of this before they met up again.

Brighton sat through most of her classes in a complete daze. She felt as if she were stepping on a wet kitchen sponge every time she flexed her foot. Her hair was still damp, and she couldn't get warm since the encounter with the rain this morning. Every window framed the same scene of tree branches bending in surrender to the unrelenting weather. She tried concentrating on the notes she was taking during her American Literature class. While she mindlessly traced the pale blue lines in the margins of her notebook, she couldn't help but think about the latest news story and the circumstances surrounding the situation.

Brighton checked the clock on the wall, her watch, and phone as if monitoring all three sources of time would accelerate the rest of class. She was looking forward to study hall in the library. There was some research she needed to do. As soon as the bell rang, she gathered her books and darted to the door. She received an irritated look from the teacher as she slid past her and the other students, who were leisurely collecting their things and making their way to class. There was no urgency, but no one else had reason to be alarmed. Brighton's speculation of pure coincidence was proving to be less and less of an explanation. What she needed to do was try to wrap her head around what exactly was unfolding in her life and town.

When she and Kate became friends six months ago, she welcomed the idea of hanging out with someone who had an interesting, colorful past. Kate didn't focus on the mundane details of ordinary teenage life. Instead of discussions of family trips to the beach, Kate passionately recounted specifics of haunted ghost tours and off-beat museums. Her eyes became wide with excitement when she described conversations with famous authors she met. Her family and their store brought a little excitement to Bradertown, and it gave Brighton a variation from the daily routine at Forest Creek High School. She wondered if the Dorns brought this much vitality to every town they lived in. So what if their best-selling item was at the center of a craze that pretty much had their whole town obsessed. It was an obsession that had been thriving for about six months. It sure made life in Bradertown lively.

Brighton thought about the repercussions if word got out that another death was linked to *My Skull Possession*. The rumors, the popularity of The Book Cellar....maybe this would make this story go nationwide or worldwide.

She knew she needed to dig deeper into the common denominators of the situation, supernatural or otherwise.

CHAPTER TEN
TOUCHÉ

Brighton piled several books around her like a fortress. She wanted the impression she was fast at work on a research paper. She opened an oversized research volume and placed her phone inside.

As she scanned through article after article about possession and the supernatural, she was surprised at what she found—or more like whom she saw. As she jotted down the name and address, someone elbowed the large book that was balanced in front of her. It hit the table with a thud, prompting everyone around her to look over. Leaning over with her hair just grazing the table top, Kate whispered to Brighton.

"Meet me in the locker rooms right after study hall."

"I thought you were in class. What are you doing here?"

They didn't have study hall together, and Brighton was sure the librarian would be over any second to reprimand both of them for breaking all of the cardinal rules of the library. Just as she heard the slow dragging of a chair against the floor, Kate disappeared as quickly as she popped up a few seconds earlier. She gave a quick wave and darted out the door. No one came over to reprimand Brighton as she realized study hall was nearing the end of the period. She gathered her books and folded the paper on which she scribbled the contact info. *Orwin's Antiques and Curiosities.*

As soon as the students filed out of the library, Brighton hurried over to the locker rooms. There were no gym classes this late in the day, so the gym was silent. The cavernous open space echoed every little sound, mainly the rain pelting the roof. Just as Brighton was about to push open the door to the girl's locker room, she felt a tap on her back.

"Hey, we can stay out here. I didn't want to talk in front of everyone, you know?" Kate whispered.

"Sure, what's going on? Why are you whispering?" Brighton was still a little annoyed from this morning when Kate acted like everything wasn't such a big deal.

"So, I wanted to let you know that I texted my dad this afternoon. I'm sorry I even said anything late last night about the crash and book correlation. My dad doesn't want to make a big deal about it. It turns out he was listening to the police scanner and heard the news about the accident. From the description of the vehicle, it sounded like a customer from earlier in the night. He told me he thought it might be him, and of course I asked him what he bought.

"What is that supposed to mean? And why does your dad listen to police scanners?"

"Yeah, weird, right? Well, anyway, I have to admit I was curious. I mean, the police said it looked as if the guy was run off the road intentionally. It could be road rage or some other personal dispute, or maybe it wasn't that at all. There's no report back yet, regarding toxicology tests or any statements from witnesses. So, when my dad said it seemed like he remembered him from earlier in the day, I had to ask."

Brighton knew where she was going with this, but she didn't understand how Kate and her dad knew all of this information about the accident from a scanner report.

"I know, and he told you he bought *My Skull Possession*, right? I figured that, but why is your dad so insistent on having you keep it quiet? If it's such a big deal and people start making connections, the rumors are going to start again anyway."

"That's just it. My dad doesn't want that. He's the only supplier of these books. He's not even sure if he is going to carry them anymore," Kate said. Her urgent tone from the texts the night before returned. "All I'm asking you is to promise me you won't say anything, okay? The hype just seemed to be leveling off from the past few weeks, and this will cause it to return two-fold."

"No worries. I didn't say anything, and I don't plan on it."

"Oh good, thanks. So, do you want to come over after school, or I can come to your house?"

"Well, actually, I planned on going somewhere after school. I don't have a ride, so I'll take the city bus. I'm sure if I call my mom she can pick me up back at the school later on."

"Wait. Why do you have to come back to the school? Can't your mom pick you up wherever it is that you are going?"

"No, I don't feel like answering a ton of questions from her. This will be easier. Saying that I am staying late at school won't send up any red flags."

"Fair enough, but I'm coming with you. Where are we going?" Kate said in her usual cheerful, assertive voice. Brighton wasn't sure if Kate was worried she was going to run to the media or police regarding the accident, or if she didn't have anything to do after school.

"Okay, if you want to go, I'm headed across town to an antique shop."

Kate paused for a second before she responded. "An antique shop? What are you looking for?" she asked.

"It's an antique and curiosity shop," Brighton said. She didn't give too many details. That was the extent of the description Brighton was willing to share. Kate could decide if she wanted to go with her or not.

"Okay. I didn't know you were into antiques. Weird."

"I didn't know your father listened to police scanners all night."

"Touché. I have to pick up my homework and coat from my locker. I'll meet you in a few minutes at the front of the school."

As Brighton headed to her locker, she thought how ironic it was that a girl with replicas of haunted dolls and a father who may be selling books that are cursed was calling *her* weird.

CHAPTER ELEVEN
MY NAME IS ORWIN

The wipers barely did an adequate job of keeping the windows clear. Brighton rarely took public transportation. She could not wait to get her license, but she knew her mom wasn't in any rush. They didn't have another car and getting one just because she hit the driving age didn't mean it was going to happen.

Kate sat across from Brighton, leaning against the pole in front of her. The only other passengers were two older women at the very back of the bus near the doors.

"I don't like taking buses. I can't wait until one of us can drive," Kate said, crossing her arms.

Her body swayed as the driver hit a rain-filled pothole, causing her to grab onto the pole. Maybe it was her vocal distaste for public transportation that made the driver "accidentally" hit the pothole.

"The shop isn't too far away. We should almost be there. According to the address, the next stop should be close enough," Brighton said while looking down at the crumpled paper on her lap.

"Oh, great. You've never been to this shop before?"

Brighton only smiled as she gathered her things and exited the bus. Both girls didn't bother putting umbrellas up but held their bags over their heads. As the bus pulled away, Brighton was sure Kate was just as skeptical as she was about getting off at this stop. They darted across the street to the address Brighton had written down. The small, rusty sign suspended above the door creaked as it rocked back and forth. It was the correct address and name, but it didn't look like it was open. Kate frowned as she tried pulling the door, but both girls were relieved when the door squeaked as she pushed inward instead.

"Hello?" Kate yelled out. No one responded. "Someone has to be here, right? They wouldn't just leave the door open."

The room where they stood wasn't so much small as it was crowded. The surrounding clutter made it feel claustrophobic, or at best, made patrons hesitant to navigate through the shelves for fear of knocking something over.

Brighton walked around looking at the various items. She found the usual trinkets and vintage baubles that fall into the antique category. The jars of shark teeth, framed shadowbox of wishbones, and bizarre wooden nesting dolls were beyond curious.

"Um, Bright, what exactly are you looking for

here?" Kate asked as she motioned to the shrunken clay head was suspended by the swath of black hair glued to the top. She splayed her fingers in disgust as she dropped it back on to the table. "Oh, this is neat." She held up a framed oil painting of a skeleton, adorned with an exaggerated hat and fanciful dress.

"Ah, La Catrina," came a voice from behind one of the shelves. "Isn't she beautiful?" Finally, the owner of the distinct voice stepped in front of them.

"Are you familiar?" the man asked as he took the painting from Kate. He held it at arm's length, tilted his head, and stared at it. "It's just lovely, isn't it?"

"La Calavera Catrina. I'm somewhat familiar. Originated from the turn of the twentieth century, I think?" Kate said while staring at the colorful artwork.

"Of course, you know what it is," Brighton muttered under her breath.

"Ooh, you know Mexican heritage and works of art," he exclaimed.

Everything he wore was ink black, including his suit, his shirt, and his tie. The only splash of color was a candy apple red handkerchief slightly poking out of his pocket. He wore small, round wire-rimmed glasses. Brighton wasn't sure if they were useful or only for aesthetics. His face was near as round as his spectacles, and the sleeves of his coat reached down to the knuckles of his stout fingers.

"Forgive me. I was in the storage room rearranging some items, but please, look around. Everyone finds something that gets their attention," he said winking at Kate. "Are you ladies looking for anything in particular? If not, yell for me if you find something of interest. My name is Orwin."

With that, he turned to some small bottles arranged in a glass curio cabinet. It looked like some of them were half-filled with liquid, but it was hard to see the detail on all of the items unless you were up close.

The dim light barely penetrated the haphazardly placed stained glass wall sconces. The walls, covered with dark purple and red wallpaper, had a muted charcoal design running from floor to ceiling. Brighton moved closer to the wall, squinted and reached out her hand, slowly brushing the wall. She felt a presence behind her hovering, and as she turned, Orwin whispered, "Yes, it's velvet. Isn't it gorgeous?" As quickly as he appeared behind her, she then heard the clinking of bottles on the glass as he went back to rearranging his baubles. Brighton wasn't sure if she should laugh or run.

Kate moved closer, and held a hand over her mouth, her unmistakable wide grin not wholly concealed.

"I like him, Bright. Why didn't you tell me about this shop before? I've been here for almost half a year, and this is the first time we stopped by. It's the coolest. It reminds me of a lot of the shops we would find during trips with my parents." She held up a small, red ceramic skull, modeling it between her two hands.

Brighton knew this shop existed, but as a young kid, if it didn't have toys or books, she wasn't interested. While the decor of the shop was unique, and its owner had a personality to match, it still carried merchandise that fell more into the category of antiques that you would find in an ordinary antique shop. The novelties and oddities nestled among the silver trays, old tea kettles, and baby carriages fulfilled the curiosity portion of the store's namesake. There was probably nothing here her mom would buy, but she wanted to make it a point to bring her back to experience the atmosphere.

"So, you never told me what it was you needed here, Bright. I don't want to stay here all day, no matter how cool the shop is. Maybe you should ask for help?" she said.

"I've meant to get over here for a while, and I just wanted to check it out. I have a quick question for Orwin, and then we can head back to the school."

"Now what can I help you with, dear? I've overheard you say this is your first time here. Believe me. Traffic has picked up in the past few weeks. I'm never surprised to see new faces. I enjoy it. Ever since the rumors from that nasty book surfaced, I get people stopping in all the time asking if we carry it. I wish I did. I could make a fortune with it. From what I hear, there is only one bookseller in town who carries that book. I wish he would spread the wealth if you know what I mean."

Brighton didn't think now was the right time to mention it was Kate's dad who should be sharing the wealth. The glare she got from Kate confirmed that was the right choice. Brighton ran her finger over the glass case, pretending to concentrate on the random array of items inside. Brighton averted Orwin's gaze by looking around the small shop. "Oh, yeah. I wondered if you knew about that book," she said.

"If I knew about it? Oh, honey, I wish I could get my hands on it. I'm telling you, people have been asking about this crazy thing for weeks, and it's only going to get crazier."

"Why is that?" Brighton asked.

Orwin dramatically hunched over the glass case. His palms squeaked against the surface as he leaned closer to Brighton and Kate. His breathy whisper smelled like cinnamon, and Brighton stifled a laugh since there was no one else in the store to hear him. He looked around as if someone else was listening.

"Right before you came to my store, I received a phone call," he whispered. He was now leaning his elbows on the glass and placed his phone in front of them.

He tapped the cover with his index finger.

He drew both of them in, his theatrics keeping their attention. Brighton wasn't a fan of the over-the-top emphasis on every little thing he said, but she was very interested in why he was so secretive in telling them this story. She played into his melodrama and asked about the call.

"So, who called?"

It was evident by his beaming face that Orwin was delighted he sparked an interest in Brighton. Kate wasn't as impressed. She uncrossed her arms, sighed and focused her attention on a chipped nail. Orwin glanced at Kate, and when he realized she wasn't as enthusiastic of an audience as Brighton, he gave a little shoulder shrug and turned his body to face Brighton as he continued his story.

"Well, I have a friend that works with the ambulance crew. The stories he tells me about some of the calls he goes to, my word," Orwin said, pausing to shake his head.

He stood up, took the handkerchief out of his pocket, waving it and holding it to his face. Kate rolled her eyes, stepped back and scratched her head while glancing at Brighton. She wasn't buying this. Brighton knew they would have to wrap this up soon before Kate said something that would embarrass her.

"Well, did something happen? Why did he call

you?" Brighton asked, trying to keep the conversation moving.

Orwin replaced the handkerchief, and opened the case, mindlessly straightening the items inside, while continuing his story.

"So, it turns out he responded to an accident last night. I'm telling you, you cannot share a word of this, ladies," he said. "Anyway, the poor fellow in the crash didn't make it. Maybe you heard about it on the news this morning, but what you didn't hear was what they found."

Brighton knew where this was going. Her face felt warm, and her heart fluttered. Kate didn't seem concerned about her chipped nail now. It was she who helped Orwin bring an end to this climactic storytelling.

"What? What did they find, Orwin?" she asked. Brighton knew Kate was fully aware of what they found. Her mouth felt dry, and she couldn't form any words to add to Kate's question.

"That book! They found that book in the car!" Orwin slammed his hands onto the case. The bottles and containers shook as if an earthquake had just rattled the store.

"You can't discuss it," he said with great conviction. "My source could get in huge trouble if anyone finds out he was giving information about the scene of a crash. Plus, it was insensitive worrying about the contents of the car, but he couldn't help it! He couldn't! When he was looking in the car for any traces of identification, there it was, on the back seat. It must have slid out of the bag during the impact. He said all he knows is that ghoulish face stared up at him from the cover, and the whole situation was disturbing. When the media gets a hold of that, believe me, they will run with it. My phone will start ringing again. Everyone will be looking for that book."

Brighton wanted to know more. She wanted to ask Orwin about theories of an object being cursed or holding supernatural power. She knew his store was her best bet on finding someone with experience with cases such as that. Surely something he had acquired or run across over the years had a story attached to it. Brighton also knew now wasn't the best time. She needed to get home soon.

"Yes. It is bizarre, Orwin," Brighton said. "And don't worry, we won't say anything. We have to get going soon. I just wanted to bring Kate along since she hasn't been to your shop since she moved here."

Orwin seemed satisfied he held a captive audience and impressed them with his story and insider information. If he only knew she was one step ahead of him. As he walked them to the door, he paused, looking at the floor in deep thought. He turned and looked at Kate. "Sweetie, I hope you enjoyed your visit, and that you will come back again. When did you say you moved to town?"

"About six months ago. Brighton has been a great friend in helping me settle in."

"Oh, that's nice. Brighton is it?" he asked.

"Yes, Brighton Corely."

"Well, Miss Brighton Corley, you sound like you are a good friend to Miss Kate. Kate, I'm sorry, I didn't catch your last name. What was it again?" he asked. He held his finger to his ear, squinted his eyes and leaned toward Kate.

"It's Dorn. Kate Dorn."

"Well, Kate Dorn, I do hope you visit again. I have a feeling you will come back. Everyone always comes back," he giggled, returning to his cheerful demeanor.

Brighton was happy he didn't press them with any other questions. She was also relieved Kate didn't mention they already knew the unfortunate details of the accident from the night before.

"Here is my card. Call, text, or email if I can ever find something that you need. I can usually help people find exactly what they are looking for," he said, as he pressed the small black card into Brighton's hand. She looked at it and focused on the words written in raised, bright gold type.

As they reached the door, she realized that the unrelenting rain hadn't stopped. She glanced at her watch and saw they only had three minutes to get the next bus back to school.

"Well, thanks again, Orwin. You do have a great shop. I'm sure we will be in touch," she said, with one hand on the door.

Kate waited behind her, scanning the store to avoid talking to either of them.

"I'm sure you will," he said while nodding and giving her a smirk. "And thanks for not mentioning anything about what I shared with you ladies. Although, you will hear about it soon enough."

"We will? I thought you said you weren't going to say anything? You didn't want to get your friend on the EMT crew in trouble, right?" Brighton asked.

"Oh, honey, please. I'm not saying a word, but I do know someone may have leaked it to the media. There were many people at that accident scene. When word of that book got out, it made enough people scratch their head. It will make for the most sensational story, especially in this sleepy little town. I'm hoping enough of those scared, but curious types come looking this way. Everyone always thinks to look here for things like that. Even though I don't have the dreaded book, I'm hoping it will continue to drive people here."

The dreaded book. Brighton could see the intensity in his eyes when he said those words, shaking his hands in the air. Brighton also knew the firestorm this was going to cause once people heard the news that this book resurfaced again. Sure, it would make them a little uneasy, but curiosity always wins out over uneasy. She stood at the door, trying to waste another minute until the bus pulled up. They only had to run outside but wanted to stand in the rain as little as possible. Orwin tried standing on his toes to peer out the door.

"Well, there you go girls. It looks like your bus is coming down the street. Hurry now. You don't want to miss it. Thanks again for a delightful afternoon. I do hope you come back soon. It was a pleasure meeting you both. Welcome to our crazy town, Miss Kate Dorn," he yelled out the door as they dodged puddles heading to the bus. Kate stopped in her tracks and spun around to look back at Orwin. His body filled the door frame, at least five feet from the floor. When he knew he got her attention, he gave a wink and again wiggled his stubby fingers. Brighton grabbed Kate's hand and ran to the bus.

As they found two seats halfway down the aisle, they sat down sitting next to one another. The bus was more filled than just an hour ago. Kate didn't say a word as they both sat, holding on to the icy metal on top of the seat in front of them. They lurched forward as the bus pulled away, and the fluorescent lights dimmed. The wipers furiously tried to keep the view clear, and the bus filled with an earthy smell. Brighton's sneakers squeaked as she tried to position herself, so she could look at Kate. She watched as she tried pulling her jacket closed tight, knowing that it did nothing against the damp that was chilling her to the bone.

"So, that's a neat shop, right?" she asked, trying to make the conversation as light as possible. Kate turned, her wet hair tucked behind her ears. Her eyeliner smeared, but even in the pouring rain, it gave her eyes a profound, smoky effect. She stared at Brighton, and she knew what Kate was thinking.

"He knows my dad owns The Book Cellar, Bright," she whispered.

"I know. I know he does."

CHAPTER TWELVE
I KNEW YOU WOULD COME BACK

The steamy water felt soothing as Brighton let it drench her hair and pelt her back. After taking a shower, she grabbed one of her favorite sweatshirts and yoga pants from the dryer. The driving rain that she found herself in several times throughout the day instilled a chill in her she couldn't shake. The sounds of her mom clanging pots in the kitchen and the beeping sound of the oven timer echoed upstairs. She knew she still had some time before dinner was ready. Her hands effortlessly wove strands of hair until a long braid cascaded over her shoulder. She felt a pull in her lower back as she sat on her bed, legs crossed, and leaned over to stare at her phone. Brighton was about to end the attempted call when someone finally answered.

"Hello?" the voice whispered.

"Hi, Orwin, it's Brighton. We were at your store earlier," she said, her voice as quiet and subdued as possible. She wasn't sure if that was from the lump in her throat, or her attempt to not be heard by her mother.

"Ah, Miss Brighton. I knew you would be calling me, my dear."

"Do you think you and I could meet up soon?"

"Absolutely. I thought you would never ask."

Brighton hoped her mother didn't see through her story. She couldn't wait until she got her license and a car of her own. Then she wouldn't need to move heaven and earth to do something as simple as going to a coffee shop. It usually wasn't a problem, but tonight it was necessary for Brighton to go by herself. She knew the coffee shop plan was weak, but it was the only business reasonably close to Orwin's shop. She didn't love the idea of hiking three blocks to the store in the dark, but it was the only way.

"Why is your study group meeting here? Wouldn't you rather meet at Barnes and Noble at the mall?" Laura asked, staring at the storefront.

"No, this is fine. It will probably be less busy, so we can get more work done. I'll call you when I need a ride, okay?"

"Well, I guess you should go in. It's getting dark out."

Brighton had no intention of going into the small shop. While she felt uncomfortable not being truthful with her mom, Brighton didn't want to explain why she was going to Orwin's.

"You should wait inside. And who did you say is part of this study group?"

"Mom. You are the one always telling me I should expand my circle of friends, right?" Brighton watched her mother's face relax, and the look of uneasiness turned into a slight smile.

"I guess. Call me when you are ready to come home. Have a good time."

Brighton watched as the car slowly rolled away. Once she was sure her mom had left, she started the walk to Orwin's shop. She knew she didn't have too much time until the dreary day plunged into complete darkness. The rain had stopped, and that was the only reason Brighton considered this plan. The newly formed study group was a stretch. Brighton rarely hung out with anyone but Kate.

As she approached the door, she heard the creak of the hinges as Orwin came out to greet her.

"It's lovely out now, isn't it? Anything is better than that torrential rain we had. I thought it was never going to stop. Please, come inside. Let's head to the back. I don't want anyone to think we are open for business. You can't imagine the number of people that peer in the windows. Even if the closed sign is up, they will start rapping on the door if they see one single light ablaze. Follow me, dear," he said.

Brighton hesitated. For the first time, she doubted coming to the store by herself, let alone not telling anyone where she was going.

Orwin's face reflected an exaggerated frown of disappointment.

"What's wrong? I thought you wanted to talk? Please tell me you don't feel threatened by me, honey. I'm just a little round guy who likes to sell unconventional novelties. Come on. How can you not trust this?" he said while twirling around.

Brighton couldn't help but let her guard down. She laughed as she followed him through the store. Her gut instinct was usually right, and Brighton had a good feeling about Orwin from the first time she met him, but she kept her phone in hand just in case.

The deep hues throughout the store made the proximity of the walls seem even closer with the lights out. As they navigated around curio cabinets, rusty washboards, and paintings leaning against the wall, Brighton took her time as not to knock anything over. Two lava lamps served as the only source of illumination, casting slow, undulating shadows on the wall behind them. As they were about to enter the back room, she paused as he disappeared behind the fringed orange curtain. Within seconds, an apricot glow flooded the floor in front of her, and Orwin held back the sheer fabric with one hand and motioned with the other.

"My lady," he said.

The small room looked as if it once served as a kitchen, minus the typical appliances. Shelves lined two of the walls, stacked with boxes overflowing with newspapers and other documents. A small countertop jutted out from the middle of a wall, protruding into the room. The end was supported by a carved wooden post, which matched the table and chairs against the far wall. It was wide enough that it contained three small shelves, crammed with supplies. A coffee pot sat atop the counter, and a hot plate sat next to it. A tiny, cheaply-made computer desk wedged itself between the table and the far wall. A small refrigerator hummed underneath the counter. No space went unused in this little nook of the building.

"I know, it is a little messy, but this is my office. There is a method to my madness. I know where everything is located," Orwin said while rifling through some of the folders stacked on the desk. "Here, please, take a seat. Can I get you some coffee or tea?"

"I'm fine, thank you. So what are all of those boxes? Just newspapers?"

Some of the rectangular boxes had lids, but she could still see magazines and newspapers sticking out of the sides.

Orwin finished filling the coffee pot with water, its red light illuminated waiting for the coffee to brew. He opened one of the lids and took something out of the box. It turns out that it wasn't a past edition of the local tabloid, but the paper was used to wrap and protect an item. He carefully placed it on the table and deliberately peeled back the crumbling paper. Preserved in this box was a chipped, ceramic chalice. Brighton picked it up and turned it in her hands. It wasn't ornate, heavy, antique, or unusual at all. She held it up under the dim overhead light, staring at it as the room filled with the scent of caramel-flavored coffee. The coffee pot hissed, and Orwin grabbed a mug filling it with the hot liquid. He sat down at the table, inhaling the steam rising from his cup.

"Are you sure?" he said motioning to the table.

"No, really, I'm fine."

"Oh, no, not the coffee, dear. Although, I will admit that it is quite good—it's caramel. I meant the chalice you are holding. Are you sure you want to know what *that* is?" he asked, strumming his fingers alongside the mug.

"It looks like an old ceramic from a yard sale."

"You are correct. It does look unassuming, but this little bugger has a story attached to it." Orwin placed his mug on the table, grabbed both lapels, and wiggled in his chair. He was settling in for another of his dramatic stories.

"So, for years I mainly focused on antiques. The common items people hunt for, while leisurely strolling through typical antique shops. You always hear these stories of people finding treasures among the trash," he said sarcastically, throwing his hands in the air. "Believe me. That rarely happens. It usually works out that someone thinks a rundown old trunk would look great in a living room, so for them, it is a great find. The fact of the matter is that it isn't necessarily rare, and it isn't necessarily unique. Over time, I began seeking out some different items. I started doing research, scouring blogs and fan websites of the supernatural. If there was a hint someone had an experience with a doll, or a mirror or a vase that seemed to be the start of an unfortunate turn of events, I was sure to try to get my hands on it."

"But how often could you come across something like that?"

"You would be surprised. Just check out eBay. People are trying to unload things like that all the time. Are they all telling the truth? Probably not. But I feel it is always worth checking into."

He picked up his coffee, slurped and exhaled with satisfaction. "Anyway, this little guy right here," he said, sitting upright in his chair. "A woman called me one day and asked if I was interested in buying a haunted vase. Again, I get calls like this all the time, but you'll never know unless you look into it. So, I went to her house out in the country. She was kind enough, but she looked troubled when she came to the door. Lived on her own, didn't seem like she had much in the old farmhouse. She thrust this damned thing into my hands. 'I don't want any money. Please take it!' she said. Orwin held the chalice, weighing it carefully in his hand.

"Why didn't she want it? Did she say?"

"No, not really. The woman said she bought it at a yard sale. She said it only brought her bad luck. Something about her cattle kept getting out of the fence, her husband died, and she kept hearing strange noises in her house."

"What kind of noises?"

"She said she heard voices," he whispered. He got up and poured himself some more coffee. "If you ask me, I think the old woman was a little batty. But I took it from her anyway. I haven't heard from her since," he said.

Brighton looked at the burnt orange ceramic piece in front of her a little differently now. What if it did bring the woman terrible luck? She wondered if it really could be the cause of the woman's ill fortune.

"Not such a boring little piece now, is it?" he said with a satisfied grin on his face. He reached over and held it at eye level. "It never seemed to bring me any problems, thankfully. I think the poor woman had a series of unfortunate events, and she associated it with buying this piece of junk," he said, pushing the chalice to the back of the table.

"But what about hearing voices? Don't you think that was strange?" Brighton agreed the other circumstances could have been construed as a string of bad luck, but the fact that the woman heard voices unnerved her.

"As I said, I wasn't too sure of her mental stability in the first place, if you know what I mean. I find something crazy on eBay, hoping it will bring traffic into my store, and it flops. There have been a few cases where I didn't sleep well at night due to some of my acquisitions. When we have more time, I'll tell you about them."

"I would love to hear about it. What did you do with those things?" Brighton asked.

"Those I unloaded very fast. Believe me. There is a market for it. It's a little dark and bizarre if you ask me, but there are buyers out there. Enough about my silly little shop of horrors, tell me about Ms. Kate," he said, emphasizing her name.

"There's not much to know. She and her family have lived here for less than a year. We are close."

"She seems nice. Now that father of hers is another story. All I know is that I was the only game in town when it came to unusual gifts. A quaint little bookshop opens up, and they are the only ones who have access to this odd book. I'm sure Mr. Dorn didn't expect to sell something that caused such a stir. The fact is it *is* causing a stir. People are intrigued, and they want a copy of it. Do they think something is going to happen to them? Probably not, but the very slight chance that it could, makes it exciting and terrifying. People love that. If I take that ceramic, put a description underneath it about its so-called history, I guarantee you it will sell."

"I don't think the Dorns intended on impacting your business."

"I'm not too sure of that. I paid a visit to Pat Dorn at his cute little shop. I discussed buying some of the stock of *My Skull Possession* at a hefty price and making it available at my store. He wanted no part of it. He said the author only wanted the book sold out of The Book Cellar. I'm not sure if Kate knows that story, but when I pieced together who she was, I thought maybe she had an ulterior motive coming here with you," Orwin said.

He seemed irritated, and that was not Brighton's intention. She was unaware of the meeting of the two business owners, but she was sure Kate had no idea who Orwin was.

"Orwin, listen, I'm sorry if I made you upset, or if you think there was some other motive for coming to see you today. All I know is that there is this book, and many people have read it, and nothing happened. Three people read it and died. They weren't sick. They weren't old, they just died. I still have a hard time believing any of the crazy stories, but I am also curious as to what is going on."

Orwin reached across the table and gripped Brighton's hands. He gave her a firm squeeze and lowered his head to stare directly into her eyes. His voice was a low, emphatic whisper, filled with conviction. "That's because, Miss Brighton, this town may be dealing with something that has a true evil connection, or it may be a bizarre coincidence that is making book sales soar. Either way, when more people from out of town hear the story, I want them to say they are coming to Bradertown and heading right to a fantastic little antique and curiosities shop."

"But if you think there is a slight chance that *My Skull Possession* has a connection to those deaths, why would you want it in your store? Why do you even want it around you?"

"Oh, sweetie, I don't want to read it, and I don't want to keep it. I want to sell it," he said, rubbing his fingers together. "As you know by now, I had my share of strange and bizarre baubles and bits, and I'm still here. I'm not going to let a little book scare me now." He looked down at the strobe light flashing on his phone.

"Excuse me, I need to take this, I have the store number forwarded to my mobile." As he proceeded to take the call, Brighton indicated she would wait out in the shop. As her eyes became adjusted to the darkness, she walked over to the only source of light. As the lava lamps slowly undulated, Brighton looked at the raven perched on a stand next to it. She ran her fingers over the glossy feathers and leaned in for a closer look. As she realized that this bird was once real, she wiped her hands on her pants.

Nestled behind the beady-eyed creature was a square metal box. As she pulled it out and brought it into view of the faint, red glow, she saw the small crank on the side. It looked like a jack-in-the-box toy. The metal was rusty and corroded. Brighton slowly turned the handle, anticipating the click and pop of a puppet jumping out of the top. She waited for the surprise as the small music box slowly came to the end of the song, but nothing appeared. She kept turning the handle, and it just repeated the song without unhinging the lid. As she placed it back behind the raven, she jumped back as a small clown puppet thrust out of the top. Brighton's heart raced, and she laughed at the threadbare clown shaking, perched atop a wavering spring. She wondered what the story was behind that toy.

As she looked at a wire birdcage slowly swaying above her, she heard Orwin droning on in the back room. She knew she had to go soon but wanted to see him before she headed out. The hair stood up on her arm as an icy chill whisked by, but she thought Orwin said the front door was secured. She walked to the entrance of the store and saw that the door was still locked. With no windows along the walls, she assumed it must have been a draft in the old building. As she returned to the counter, the stream of frigid air was gone. She hoped Orwin would wrap up his call soon. As she tried to make out the year on an old poster on the wall, he dramatically stepped back in.

"Look, I have to get going. Thanks for talking to me," Brighton said while heading to the door.

"Is someone picking you up here? You can wait inside until they arrive."

"I have to walk a few blocks. It was kind of late, so I told my mom I was meeting a study group at the coffee shop. I told her to pick me up there."

"Aw, did you think she wouldn't approve of getting dropped off at some weird guy's place? Come on, sweetie. I'll at least drop you off at the coffee shop. Just give her a call and tell her you will be outside."

"It's okay. I'm sure the store is still open. I'll hang out in there until she shows up."

"Listen to me. You are better off staying outside," Orwin said as they made their way to the adorable Mini Cooper parked in front of the store. "They don't have the most pleasant workers, to begin with. I tried buying something the other day, and this crusty old man gave me a hard time."

"A hard time because you wanted coffee?" Brighton asked, sliding into the midnight black leather seat.

Orwin strummed his fingers against the shifter, his silver rings tapping as he hesitated before pulling away from his store. Brighton fell back into her seat as he suddenly shifted and rushed down the street. The engine whirred, and Orwin adjusted the volume on the radio.

"No. No. Not coffee," he said, breaking the awkward silence. "I was interested in something he was selling, and he didn't allow me to buy it. But it's okay, I plan on going back there when someone else is around. They can't all be miserable. Anyway, you have a good night, my dear. We will talk soon," he said while stopping in front of the coffee shop.

After several minutes, her mom finally pulled up. Brighton realized Orwin didn't leave and was waiting down the road. She smiled when she saw the sporty little coupe fly into reverse, complete a U-turn, and head down the street.

"How did everything go?" her mom asked. "Did you get much work done?"

"We just did some brainstorming, but it was very constructive. I'm glad I ended up going."

"So Kate didn't go?"

Brighton didn't answer right away. She was unsure how her mom knew Kate wasn't with her, and Brighton couldn't remember if she mentioned anything before. She kept her silence.

"Brighton? Honey? I asked why she didn't go. Kate dropped by the house looking for you, and I told her you went with some friends to get some work done."

Brighton was happy she didn't say anything to incriminate herself.

"Yeah, she's not working on this project with me. I guess I forgot to tell her we were meeting tonight. Anyway, how was work?" Brighton said, trying to shift the conversation.

After they arrived home, she told her mom she was tired and headed to her room. It was pretty late, and she needed to complete her real homework before she crashed for the night. As she finished the last of her essay questions, she tossed her notebook and papers on the floor and reached over for the light. Her mind started processing the events of the day, and she attempted to make sense of what happened. It only took a few minutes as exhaustion led her to fall asleep faster than recent nights.

CHAPTER THIRTEEN
ANOTHER DEATH, ANOTHER BOOK

"It was on the news, and it was in the paper. Everyone is posting about it on Facebook. They found the book in his car, and get this—he didn't even read it. He only bought it. There is something freaky about that book."

Brighton listened as two girls standing at the locker next to her gossiped about what was shaping up to be the hottest topic at Forest Creek High School. The whole town was buzzing about it.

Whether it was Orwin's call to one of the local stations or another source that leaked it from the accident scene, the word was out. Thomas Stricklan was in a terrible accident, and a copy of the book was found in the car. Brighton still thought it was a stretch.

Brighton leaned against the rows of lockers, as students scrambled to their classes. She knew she only had a few minutes but wanted to see what the Forest Creek Herald had online.

> Fatal motor vehicle accident: Tom Stricklan of Forest Creek died late last night after his vehicle left the roadway. Crews responded to the crash, but Stricklan was pronounced dead

at the scene. No evidence of impaired driving found, but witnesses say another vehicle may be involved. This story is developing.

Brighton wondered how that article created a buzz. There was no mention of the book found in the car. The story didn't even elaborate on the fact the other vehicle pushed Stricklan off the road. It must be because it is still under investigation. It wasn't until she scrolled down that she saw it. The comments read:

Scrgrl: I heard he had the book in the car. My Skull Possession.

Scott567: The book didn't kill him, he ran off the road. Probably drugs.

Scrgrl: Nope. Totally because of that book. Like, all these people that are reading it are dying!

JimB: Where can I get that book?????

Scrgrl: I wouldn't read it.

The comments went on and on. She should have known by now that it's not the content of the article that perpetuates rumors; it's the trolling that follows it. That is what everyone reads online. Orwin got the word out there, but thankfully the local news didn't run with it.

"Ms. Corley, can you please come to class? Also, please put that phone away, or I will need to take it off of you," her teacher said. Brighton filed into her classroom and slid into the chair. She felt a slight tap on her shoulder. It was Kate getting her attention.

"Hey, so looks like this book isn't going away anytime soon," she whispered. "Oh and how did studying go last night?"

Kate slid back in her chair, crossing her feet at the ankles. She raised one perfectly defined eyebrow at Brighton, waiting for a response.

"We can talk about this later. I'm already in trouble for using my phone outside of class," Brighton said.

"Why didn't you tell me you were going back out to study? You never mentioned that part.

Brighton knew her studying excuse was weak. Kate was smart and very observant. They both turned forward as their teacher lowered her glasses to look at both of them.

As Brighton concentrated on the whiteboard in front of her, she dreaded explaining why she went back to the curiosity shop without Kate. She felt something close to the back of her head but refused to turn around.

"Let me know if you have any other adventures planned after school," Kate whispered.

Chapter Fourteen
Lorna

As Brighton approached the entrance to the cemetery, she debated as to whether or not she should take the shortcut on her way to Kate's. In the interest of time, she decided it was still light enough. Brighton adjusted her backpack and planned to make it a brisk walk along the path. As she neared the halfway mark of the road, a single ray of sunlight pierced through the branches of one of the maple trees.

Its blinding light illuminated the marble of one of the headstones. Brighton had never noticed it before, but the laser-like focus made it unavoidable. Centered in the middle of the tombstone was a small gleaming oval. Brighton tried to make out what it was as she approached the gravestone, but the light bounced off only allowing the silhouette to come into view. The stone wasn't adjacent to the road as it sat a few rows back. Brighton wanted to get to Kate's house, but she was intrigued by the brilliance of the reflection. She felt uncomfortable walking through the graveyard without staying on a path. The intrusion of crossing and walking over graves felt disrespectful. There was no other way to access the markers that were located a few rows back, so Brighton gingerly stepped through the grass leading to the curious reflection.

As she reached the marble monument, her body interrupted the afternoon sunlight. The remnants of the day felt good. Brighton assumed it was marble, but realized the dark headstone was granite with gleaming blue and silver pearl-like crystals. It looked more expensive than the other monuments surrounding her. It was then that she saw the small, silver cameo in the center, framing a black and white photo of a beautiful woman with her hair pulled back neatly into a bun. She shifted to the side and realized the sun was bouncing off of this picture. The combination of the pearl-like flecks, silver framing, and glass overlay definitively exaggerated the light. She ran her hand over the cold stone and turned to make her way back to the path. Just as she was about to walk away she noticed something. A few graves down sat a less opulent headstone that had a small flower in front of it and a miniature lamb on top of the gravestone. Brighton crouched down to look at the words inscribed into the gray stone.

Abner Karender b. 1924 d. 1965
Lorna Rellim Karender b. 1925 d. 2015
Beloved daughter b. 1955   d. 1965

Brighton ran her finger over the carved stone, wondering how she never saw it before.

As she made her way out of the cemetery in a trance like state, she couldn't get the image of the small, white lamb out of her mind. She didn't know who Lorna was, but in 1965 it seemed like she dealt with a lot of heartache. Brighton couldn't wait to share her discovery with Kate, but before heading to her house, she turned around once more. The focused ray of light only moments ago beckoned her to stray from the path, but now it was gone.

Before she mentioned anything about the cemetery, Brighton knew she had to address her return visit to see Orwin.

"I don't understand why it was such a big secret that you were going back there," Kate said, resting her head against the wall behind her bed. She fiddled with a small lacquered box, its metallic panels shining on both sides of the cube.

"I'm sorry. I got the feeling that Orwin wanted to talk to me alone. Plus, I still wanted to pick his brain, hoping he would share some of his stories with me. There are some interesting details attached to a few of the things he was selling. Weird things, like the stuff you collect," Brighton said. She didn't want Kate to be mad at her. "He had a strange picture from this woman..."

"Stop." Kate said.

"What?" Brighton replied, shocked at the abruptness.

"Just stop, okay? I understand your curiosity, and I have to admit the store is very cool. You realized Orwin figured out who I was. He had a problem knowing my dad has the bookstore. Instead of finding out what the issue was, you didn't even mention it."

"Look, I think he's jealous about the success of your dad's store in recent months."

"Oh, I know he is."

"You do? I thought you were wondering what the problem was?"

"I did. So when I got home, I asked my dad if he was ever at Orwin's Antiques and Curiosities. He explained that he was but also that Orwin approached him a few times, pleading with my dad to sell some of his inventory. He pretended he was looking for an assortment of titles, but he was most interested in acquiring copies of *My Skull Possession*. My dad told Orwin that the distribution of the book was exclusive to his store. Dad tried to explain to him that it wasn't up to him."

Brighton was relieved they were on the same page as to why Orwin seemed cautious when around Kate. She felt that eased some of the tension between them.

"So, what do you think about those names?"

Brighton asked. When she arrived at Kate's house, she couldn't wait to tell her about what she found. "There has to be a connection. It's strange that I happened to walk by at that time, drawn into the area. Otherwise, I would never have seen that name."

"I think it's a coincidence. Although the last name is the same, there's no mention of Elle. Plus, it looks like they had a daughter who died young."

"I know, but what if there is a connection? Maybe we can find out if there are any other relatives around. What has your dad said about the author again?" Brighton asked.

"I told you, it's not the author. The guy dropping off the books is just the contact person. I guess the book has been in his family for years, and he is doing his best to make some money from something written years ago. That's the end of it."

Kate tossed the small box that was the focus of her attention over to Brighton. "Maybe you can solve it."

Brighton wasn't sure if she meant the puzzle or the fascination with *My Skull Possession*. "This puzzle?" she asked, pointing to her hand.

"Yes. My dad got it from a conference he attended last week. He received it as a gift from an illusionist he knows.

"An illusionist? What kind of conference was your dad at?" She laughed.

"It was just an independent bookseller's convention. Some of those bookstores sell other novelties besides books. I guess this guy was into magic," she said, shrugging her shoulders.

Brighton studied the small box and recalled that it looked like a puzzle she used to play with as a kid. She turned the top three times to the right, then twice to the right. After pushing down on the cover, she was able to slide it off gently. Inside, mirrors lined the walls of the box, and a small silver skull was attached to the bottom. She looked at it and threw it over to Kate.

"Okay, did you set that up? A skull? Really?"

Kate peered into the small case. She placed it on her dresser. "I promise you. I didn't know anything was in there. My dad gave it to me and said I should try to solve it. I thought it was a puzzle."

"A puzzle with a pretty ironic surprise," Brighton said, as she walked over and stared at the tiny skull shining on the table.

"Okay, well, maybe we can go back and talk to Orwin. He might know something more about this Rellim name. Let's check out his hours."

Brighton hoped Orwin wouldn't be irritated when she returned with Kate. She wasn't the one who refused to share any of the books. Just as she was about to bring it up to Kate, she noticed Kate dropped her phone on the bed and held her hands to her face.

"What's wrong?"

"Here, look," Kate said, picking up her phone and handing it to Brighton.

Staring up at her was the account for Orwin's shop. The latest post is what shocked her.

Greetings to my loyal and valued customers. I am happy to say I just received a few copies of My Skull Possession. With every purchase over $50, your name will be entered to win a free copy. Come and try your luck at winning the most sought-after book everyone is dying to read!"

Brighton stared at Kate. "How did he get those books?"

"I guess my dad finally caved. Whatever. He got what he wanted. Who knows how many people will see the post." No one knows if anyone goes to his website. He doesn't have many followers. I hear my mom downstairs. Let's run over and find out for ourselves."

"The antique store? Oh, come on Kate. That's the guy who has been bugging your father for some of the books to sell. Why am I taking you there?" her mom asked.

"It sounds like Dad gave in because he has some of them in stock. I'm just curious what kind of turn out he has after he made that announcement!"

Kate's mom was silent as they drove across town. As they approached the turn, they noticed a line of people snaked around the corner. People stood in the slow-moving line leading into Orwin's shop.

"Mom, just wait here. I won't take too long. Brighton, are you coming with me?" she said, her eyes urgently staring from the store back to Brighton.

"Sure," she said, jumping out of the car.

They surveyed the customers who slowly made their way closer to the entrance. Filling out the line were parents with teens, couples, and some older men and women. A few young kids ran around chasing each other as the line snaked its way along the side of the building. Brighton tapped one of the teenage girls on the shoulder.

"Excuse me, what is everyone waiting in line for?" she asked, already knowing the answer.

"They have that book. You know, the one some people read and it scared them to death? It's pretty hard to get now, and Orwin is giving away free copies. I'm dying to read it," she said, laughing, as she nudged her friend waiting next to her.

Brighton rolled her eyes, and pushed her way to the front of the line, pulling Kate behind her. She searched over the sea of people until the top of Orwin's head came into view. He yelled from the counter as he handed over a bag to one of the customers.

"Can't talk now ladies, but thanks for dropping

by. I only got a few copies, but look at the response," he said, waving his hand feverishly. "We can catch up tomorrow."

Brighton could tell Orwin was elated. His goal of having one of the sought-after books in his possession and making it available to his customers came true. She just hoped this wasn't followed by any negative press this time.

Brighton and Kate waved and watched as he returned to tending to the line in front of him. Everyone was purchasing in hopes of winning a copy of the book. Brighton realized at that moment how much people loved being scared, but more importantly, getting something hard to acquire.

Kate's mom gave her watch an exaggerated glance and pulled away with a bit more intensity than her usual driving habits as Kate and Brighton returned to the car.

"You know, your father didn't sell any books to Orwin. He or someone he knows must have purchased them and are now re-selling. That's not great business practice."

Kate decided it wouldn't be the best time to mention Orwin's customers had to spend at least fifty dollars to *possibly* get a copy of *My Skull Possession*.

"Yeah, weird. I'll have to find out how he actually got the copies," she said. "It's too busy now, so let's just go home."

Brighton didn't say anything. She continued to stare out the window, watching Orwin's store disappear in the distance. The line of people still reached to the corner. Brighton thought about a young guy who ecstatically ran out of the store, taking a selfie while holding a ticket, he might be one of the owners of *My Skull Possession* if his name was picked. It could also be a lottery the winners would most certainly regret.

CHAPTER FIFTEEN
DREAD AND PARALYSIS

Brighton arrived home to find her mom already back from work. She felt comforted by the aroma of her mom's famous chicken noodle soup simmering on the stove.

"I'm surprised you aren't talking about the accident," her mom said, catching Brighton off guard. She didn't even lift her head and stared intently at her bowl in front of her. She knew her mom would continue. "I still don't buy into it, but even some of my co-workers were discussing it today. I'm sure Kate's parent's store will be busier than ever now."

"So, you *do* find it strange? The accident, the book, all of those other people?"

Her mom stood and put water on for tea. Brighton nodded as her mom held up a small foil pack of chamomile tea leaves.

"Oh, honey. You know how I feel about this. I think many customers are victims, but they are only victims of a pretty slick marketing idea. I think more theories and ideas are being passed around on social media, rather than facts reported."

"My question is why all those deaths were unexplained, and they just so happened to read the book."

"It sounds somewhat suspicious. Did anyone ever interview or talk to the families of those who died? Did the information come from a friend of a friend of the family?" she asked, pouring the boiling water into two glass mugs. The comforting aroma of chamomile swirled around Brighton. She held the cup to her face, inhaling the fragrant steam.

"I didn't personally talk to anyone in the family. That would be weird since I didn't know them that well. I do know some of the kids in school had a connection."

As the words came out of her mouth, she realized how unstable the stories sounded. She wondered how it got so out of control. Every time she talked to her mom about this, she always looked at it from a different angle, and it caused Brighton to question the validity of the reports.

"The soup was great, Mom. I'm going to get some work done and hopefully go to bed a little early."

"Okay, sweetie. I'm just trying to paint the picture in a little more realistic view."

Brighton straightened her room and turned on the string of lights she had running across the ceiling. She turned a small lamp on that was next to her bed. After looking at her planner, Brighton realized that none of her assignments were due the next day. She checked her phone for messages, and scrolled through Facebook and

Instagram, looking for any breaking news. There was none.

Orwin had his website updated, reflecting the winners of the book contest. A few of the customers must have hung around his store. There was a picture with Orwin and one of the winners. He held the book out in front of him, with a sarcastic, scared look on his face. This gesture made Brighton laugh out loud. She wasn't tired, and she had no plans on doing anything constructive this evening. After talking to her mom, Brighton felt a little more rational.

Brighton reached under her bed for the book. She figured she might as well join the ranks of everyone else to see what all of the hype was about surrounding *My Skull Possession*.

> If I succumb to the evil that surrounds me, if I let the darkness into my soul, I will be at ease knowing that I will not be unheard. The document of my account is so others will understand what torturous suffering I have endured. They think me mad that my fanciful descriptions are created only by the deep recesses of my convoluted mind. I describe what I see at night. When the world is unconscious with slumber, when the stars pierce the black of night with poignant specks of light—it is then that my terror begins.

Brighton shifted on her bed and tried adjusting the pillows behind her. As she reclined and attempted to make herself more comfortable, she felt it. A cold draft caressed the side of her face and neck, immediately causing her to jump to her feet. She touched her hand to her cheek and looked around the room. That is when she noticed the long curtain softly billowing against the windowsill. As she slowly crawled over and reached out to move the fabric, she realized her mother must have opened her window to let in some fresh air. She always did that, even in the frostiest of winters. When Brighton left this morning, she knew the window wasn't opened, but she was sure her mother went around trying to get air circulating in the house. Brighton slammed it shut and lowered the curtain back into place.

"Get a grip," she said aloud.

The book was written in first person, and Brighton wondered if it was just the point of view or if it was autobiographical. The prose was a little more flowery than what she was used to reading, but it set an eerie tone early on. She looked at the window and the stationary curtain. There was no breeze blowing through her room. She retrieved her book from the floor and settled back into her bed.

> I sit in my room and wait for it to start. Like clockwork, the footsteps echo downstairs although I know nothing is touching the floor.

The sound of heavy breathing resounds in my ear yet there is nothing in my room. I close my eyes, thinking this will shut out the unwelcome thoughts and sounds, but doing this only causes me to imagine what could be making its way up the stairs to the second floor. No one else in the home can experience what I am experiencing.

Maybe I am mad. As I assure myself that these mysterious occurrences must be the result of my creative, but overactive, imagination. I open my eyes and focus on the door. It only takes a matter of seconds until the hinges begin to squeak. Ever so slowly, the door inches open, its doorknob getting closer and closer to the wall. I am paralyzed with fear, and I know it does not end there. A shadowy figure fills the doorway, but I can't make out the features. The faceless entity shifts into different forms as it floats above the floor. I could scream, but it is of no use. It will still move closer.

I watch as a shadow creeps along the wall, taking the shape of a pointed cloaked figure. The comfort I sought by leaving the small oil lamp ablaze is now the very thing allowing me to confirm the unwelcome visitor has returned. It reaches the foot of my bed and stops. What does it want? My pleading and tears do not make it disappear. My prayers dissolve, unanswered, into the blackened atmosphere. This time I think it will stay positioned at my feet. I no longer question as the fearsome presence navigates around the corner of my bed. Slowly, it folds itself closer to my face, as if it is looking for something. The air around me is cold, my body trembles. Why don't I flee you ask? Why don't I escape from this terror through the open door? I can't. Something is telling me that the horror I feel now will pale in comparison if I try to escape. The apparition makes no sound as it grows closer to me. It is lingering near my bed. My heart feels as if it will explode out of my chest. There is no warm breath, no raspy voice, no haunting sound as the figure is near my face. A sickening feeling overcomes me as I feel an icy touch on my hand and then my face and throat. It never attempts to harm me, but the bitter chill lingers on my skin, and I can feel it in my bones. Tears stream down my face, and in the faintest whispering, I cry that I am so scared. The figure slowly fades, as if it listened to my pleas, but it re-materializes in the rocking chair near my bed. It is there that it sits watching, not moving until it disappears and the chair rocks back and forth. I am afraid to get out of bed, and I am scared to go to sleep. I keep telling myself that it is all a nightmare. A nightmare that reoccurs and revisits me every night.

It started as a faint sound, and every night progressed, getting closer. When it finally reached my room, I thought my heart would explode. Could no one in my home see what I am seeing? Can they not hear my heart beating out of my chest? If I am not mad, I swear this will drive me insane. It is only then that I drift off to sleep.

I awake the next morning and stare at the rocking chair. It is not moving, nor is it occupied. Every morning, when the sun streams through my window, and I hear nature begin to start the day, I tell myself that my nightmare is trying to take control of me, but I can't let it win. Only I know it's not merely a nightmare and that tonight the same visitor will return. Dread and paralysis are all

I know in the late hour. Oh, how I wish this could end. How I hope I could understand the meaning of this. My great fear is to what progression this will lead. What is being sent to me by this dark messenger? These questions ring empty, for no one will believe such exaggeration from a child. I'm not sure how much to which I can withstand.

After reading several more chapters, Brighton closed the book and held it on her lap. It was creepy, but she didn't think she would have too much trouble falling asleep tonight. Brighton placed the book on the floor next to her. As she retreated under her comforter, she stared at the small white lights lining the perimeter of her room. She figured her eyes were heavy, and her mind was trying to unwind, but she could have sworn the lights were twinkling. A slow, pulsing flicker that made her pop out of bed. She carefully checked the bulbs when she added the string of lights the other day. Brighton decided against twinkling lights, thinking it would be a distraction when she was trying to create a sanctuary to relax. Right now, they were not static. Brighton threw back the blankets, got out of bed and decided to check the connections. It was then that she heard a slight buzzing sound and her bedroom plunged into darkness. She felt her way over to her bed and turned on the small lamp on her nightstand. It was staying on for the remainder of the night. As she slipped back into bed, she knew sleep would not come quickly.

"Rational, rational," she repeated squeezing her eyes tight. She did hang the lights the other day. They got their use as Christmas decorations. Every year when they would drag boxes of ornaments and strings of lights out of the attic, there was always at least one strand they couldn't get to work. It wasn't strange then, it shouldn't bother her now, she thought. Her breathing was heavy, and she tried her calming techniques again. Her tee shirt clung to her body from the sweat. She had to remember she did just close the door and window. Like her mom always said, no air circulation is bad for you. She once again jumped out of bed, pushed open the window and rested her elbows on the windowsill. The cool rush of air felt like she got a reboot.

Brighton pressed her head against the screen and inhaled deeply. As she returned to bed and tried to fall asleep, her rationalization wasn't working too well. Brighton knew it was probably a mistake to read the book right before bedtime. She thought about the issue with the lights, reassuring herself it was due to an electrical malfunction. Sounds of footsteps echoed in her mind, but she knew there was no one in her hall. As she looked at the floor, *My Skull Possession* was staring back at her, beckoning her to continue reading. She thought she shoved it under the bed, but maybe she kicked it when getting up to open the window.

After lying in bed for almost an hour, she knew she couldn't fall asleep. The book set her mind in motion.

She sat at her desk and decided to do a little research on her computer. There were tons of Facebook posts and blog analysis about *My Skull Possession*. She followed the attached links that brought up eBay-haunted items for sale.

"Ugh," she said out loud, reading through tons of descriptions from dolls to watches.

One post read: "After finding the doll in an old trunk, my son is afraid to sleep in his room alone. He talks about an old man that lives in our basement, and we have all heard laughing. You can hear what sounds like footsteps in the attic. I am not responsible for anything that may or may not happen when in possession of this doll."

Brighton clicked on the next entry. "This watch is stopped at 11:29 p.m., supposedly the exact time the previous owner died. I would feel unexpected temperature drops when wearing, even in 80-degree weather. I cannot guarantee the same experience I had nor am I responsible for any you may experience."

"Ok, I didn't need to read that," Brighton said, continuing to speak out loud. She returned to scouring Facebook posts of people arguing whether or not an item could become possessed. This next article she clicked on made her feel more at ease.

"If history has taught us anything, it's that the legend of a haunted thing is good for business. It's been good for the Hope Diamond, which is said to bring death and heartache to whoever possesses it," read one of the selections. "Using the label of haunted is a weirdly successful way to sell old dolls, shoes or mirrors."

She laughed as she scrolled down and found an image of Robert the Doll. It explained in detail how the doll was said to show up in front of windows on its own. "Why would Kate want that thing?" Brighton groaned. She ended her research for the night as her eyelids began to feel heavy.

CHAPTER SIXTEEN
NO SCHOOL

Brighton awoke to the familiar chime on her phone. Six missed messages from Kate. She heard a light knock on her bedroom door and saw her mom's head peeking in.

"Hey sleepy head, I tried waking you before, but you were still out cold. I have to head out, but I'm sure you know already."

"Know what?" Brighton said. She tried to stretch her neck by slowly pulling her head to one side. At some point, she must have dozed off in front of her computer before she retreated to bed.

"No school. That will make for a nice, long weekend. I have to run. Text me if you need anything. Love you," Laura said, blowing her daughter a kiss.

Before Brighton could respond and try to clear up this confusion, her mom began to shut the door. Just as quickly, she popped her head back in again.

"What did you do to your lights? Didn't like them after all?" her mom said looking up at the ceiling.

Brighton held her phone in her hand, trying to make sense of this morning. Above her, the white lights with the same color cord were tacked to the ceiling, but where each connection met, it was unplugged. She remembered being worried about the lights, but she didn't remember unplugging each strand.

"I think there is a short in one of them, so I thought it would be safer with no current," she yawned.

"I guess that makes sense. It's a nice touch to your room. Anyway, I'll call you later."

She decided to return the missed calls and texts from Kate.

"Hey, Kate. So, what is going on? Why is school canceled today? I mean, I'm not complaining, but your message said it was a water main break?"

"So they say. I don't know. Personally, I think the district wanted to keep the rumor mill at bay. The huge gathering at Orwin's yesterday and the recent accident is all everyone is talking about. Maybe they think if students aren't congregating, rumors won't spread as fast."

"That doesn't make any sense. It's social media that is propelling this. It will give kids, at least, more time to stew and spread more rumors. I think that defeats the purpose. Maybe the school does have a water main break. We should walk by later and check. Nevertheless, we get a long weekend. I can stand to go back to bed right about now anyway."

"Really, what were you doing up so late?"

"I couldn't sleep. And I started reading *My Skull Possession*."

"You did? Finally! Hey, I'm still talking to you, so you must still be alive," Kate joked.

"Very funny. No, it's fine. The book is a little weird, and it probably didn't help reading it so late at night. But, yeah, I'm fine."

Brighton didn't tell her about the slight breeze and the issue with the lights. She was sure it was just coincidence but didn't feel like explaining it away again. As always, in the light of day, she felt more assured that everything was okay.

"I told you it's no big deal. Unless you just weren't affected yet," Kate said, laughing.

Brighton let that pass. "What did your dad say about all of this? Why did he finally give Orwin some books for his store?"

"He said he didn't want to talk about it. He was pretty upset, so I figured I wouldn't push it. I think he's sick of all of the drama surrounding the book already. He gets calls from all over the country asking who his distributor is. They get angry when my dad tells them that he's the only one contracted to sell the books. That's not to say some of those people coming into the store aren't reselling them themselves. But that's why he put a three-book limit on quantities. It is turning into a circus."

Brighton didn't know if she agreed with that. When she was there with her mom a few days ago, there were no customers in the store at all. She assumed it was busier earlier in the day and on weekends, but it didn't seem like crowds that he couldn't handle. And when he did have lines out the door, wasn't that a good thing?

"So, how does your dad get his shipment? Does the supplier send them or drop them off in person?"

"Oh yes, our supplier. The guy is weird. I mean, in the beginning, he would come into the store with boxes. Now, sometimes he sends them, sometimes he drops them off. Strange guy, really quiet. He doesn't know much about the publishing world, that's for sure. He doesn't have any business skills, either. I'm surprised my Dad agreed to work with him. He went out on a limb with this one, but it worked out well. Enough about that. I'm happy we are out of school."

Brighton agreed and planned to meet Kate later on in the day. Right now, she wanted to catch up on some sleep. Even though her room was bathed in daylight, she still found it a lot easier to fall asleep.

CHAPTER SEVENTEEN
THE MYRTLES PLANTATION

Brighton felt refreshed after catching up on some sleep. She was happy that Kate hadn't eaten lunch yet. She was starving and hurried to get ready. The walk wasn't far to the small restaurant near Kate's house. It wasn't somewhere that either of them would travel by foot at night, but having the day off gave them plenty of time to leisurely stroll to their destination to have lunch. They passed by the school and stared at a sign on the front door, stating that classes would resume on Monday. There were no utility trucks on the property, and the structure itself seemed pretty vacant. It's possible the water break issues were wrapped up by now or that they never occurred at all.

"Classes will resume Monday, hmm," Kate said as they kept walking. "Seems like they cleaned that up pretty quickly."

There were a few busy streets to cross, crowded with endless traffic. Brighton remembered why they didn't like walking this way and preferred to be dropped off. As they reached the restaurant, Brighton felt nostalgic. She frequented this place numerous times with her mom. The decor was not updated since she started eating here, but that's what made it most enjoyable. CASH ONLY signs hung on the door as you walked in. There was ample seating to accommodate a large crowd, including booths and tables. A few bar stools lined the u-shaped area near the grill. Brighton enjoyed seeing the same faces parked at these seats visit after visit. She hoped they never change a thing.

"What can I get ya?" a waitress said. She held a small pad, scribbling down a few orders. Kate looked around for a menu, and although Brighton knew there were a few circulating throughout the restaurant, most of the regulars knew what they wanted when they came into Joe's Diner and BBQ.

"I'll have pork barbecue with relish, small fries, and a small Coke," Brighton said.

Kate looked at her and rolled her eyes. "I guess I'll have the same," she said with a touch of sarcasm.

The waitress smiled and disappeared through the swinging door. Brighton knew the food would be out in no time. The limited menu allowed the service to be quick, without sacrificing the quality of the food.

"Well aren't you just the regular here," Kate said, tapping her fingers on the table.

"You've been here before. I thought you knew the menu."

"I haven't been here as many times as you, but I

128

do remember the food is great. So, you got some sleep, that's good. And you are still alive—even better. Did you read any more of the book?"

"A few more chapters. It's good. It's not a modern-day novel. I can't pinpoint the time frame yet. It's possible it's autobiographical, that is if the author was completely crazy."

Kate shifted in the booth. She twirled the end of one of the braids that rested on her shoulder. The fluorescent lights bounced off her lips shining with lip gloss the color of strawberry sorbet. She was quiet while the waitress returned with some napkins and tall, plastic tumblers.

"What did you think? Did you feel like it was the result of great storytelling, or was this author trying to tell us something?" Brighton asked.

Kate swirled the soda, not raising her head to look at Brighton and said, "I didn't read it."

Brighton was dumbfounded. She was pressured by Kate to take a copy of the book, to read it, to let her know what she thought. She could've sworn Kate wanted to reread it. "But didn't you say you wanted to..." she started saying before being cut off from Kate.

"I know, I know, I said I wanted to reread it. The truth is I never read it the first time. Sorry I didn't tell you that before."

As expected, the food came out from the kitchen

quickly. Brighton smiled at the waitress, as she picked up the ketchup bottle and hit the bottom to get some of it onto the plate.

"Okay, so you didn't read it. Why not? Why didn't you tell me?"

Kate fiddled with her earring. Her stare could bore a hole in the faded linoleum floor.

"Kate? Hello?" Brighton crumpled a napkin and tossed it at her," did you hear me?"

The chair scraped against the floor as Kate jerked closer to the table. She focused her gaze on the cup as if she were trying to levitate it. "If you must know, it was my dad. He suggested I shouldn't read it. Look, we've seen some pretty strange things in our travels, and he didn't want me getting wrapped up in this hype, I guess. I mean, it's not that he thought anything would happen, but he also didn't want me obsessing over it. I figured it was easier to let it go. I think that is what we should do."

Still no eye contact.

"Wait. Obsessing over it? I'm confused."

This was the first time she ever heard Kate waver on anything. Whenever Kate told stories describing the unbelievable trips she would take with her family, Brighton would listen to descriptions of both luxurious hotels and impressive landmarks. The souvenirs she brought back were mementos from their travels. Brighton found it a little odd that while most people returned with ornaments and books as keepsakes, Kate had a collection of oddities such as haunted doll replicas and skulls. She assumed it was her parents that encouraged maintaining a bizarre collection of trinkets, but maybe it was Kate after all.

Kate raised her head, pausing before she spoke. Brighton could see that she wanted to crawl out of the dark place she escaped to minutes before. The hesitation seemed like hours, but something was drawing her out.

"Well, you know we've bounced around a lot of places, and I became super interested in some of the local stories, history, and legends. Have you heard of the Myrtles Plantation mirror?" she said, slowly sipping her soda, and taking a bite of her sandwich. A pink haze coated the straw as she placed the frosted tumbler back on the table.

"No, but I assume I'm about to," Brighton said. The emptiness reflected in Kate's eyes disappeared. Brighton couldn't tell if they glistened from emotion or the harsh lightening.

"I won't go into all of the details, but when we visited a plantation in Louisiana, we learned of some alleged haunted objects, one being a mirror. Some members of the family died, some say it was murder, and their souls are trapped in the mirror."

Brighton smiled and focused on the crumpled straw wrapper next to her glass. She knew it sounded far-fetched, but didn't her concern about a book being possessed sound just as crazy?

Kate gripped the table and stopped with another dramatic pause. She exhaled as if she spent minutes underwater.

"Yeah, it sounds crazy. But while on the tour, we heard the legend and ghost story, then got to see the mirror. We took pictures, and when I looked at them more closely back at the hotel, I was sure that I saw handprints and an outline of a person. My parents definitely weren't as impressed as I was, but after we left the plantation, I was obsessed. I mean, I couldn't get enough information about it. I showed the pictures to anyone who would look at them; I talked to folks who grew up in the Baton Rouge area, and I couldn't stop. It freaked me out, but I needed to know more and more. My parents tried to explain that my imagination wanted to see these images, but there was an explanation. I became annoyed that they wrote me off, and I grew obsessed with research on my own. Eventually, I became overwhelmed with not only the plantation but similar stories. We needed to move a few times for various reasons, and my parents hoped moving here to a somewhat 'normal, small town' would keep me grounded."

Brighton created a small whirlpool in her soda,

splashes of cola landing on her hand. She wasn't sure how to respond and didn't expect a revelation like this in a million years. Kate, who seemed like she could have the world at her fingertips, sounded like she was trapped. Not in a physical sense but by her overactive and speculative imagination. As Brighton jabbed at the ice with her straw, she now understood that supernatural books at Kate's house, the strange artifact collection in her room and her fascination with the cemetery. It was Kate's doing, not her parents. Brighton had it all wrong.

"I guess you think I'm crazy now, right? Believe me, you're not the only one. Listen, I was so excited there were no issues when I moved here. I appreciate your friendship, and I think we're on the same page. When this whole thing started with the rumors about the book, my parents were nervous I was going to become obsessed with the whole idea. I wanted to sound like I thought it was cool, so that's why I told you I read it. That's all. I hope you'll forgive me," Kate said.

Brighton was surprised by the conversation, but she wasn't upset. Everything Kate said made sense, and she could understand how easy it was to become consumed with something. Such as thinking a book could cause you to feel sick, or make lights in your room shut off. Brighton wondered if she looked into things too closely or if she had legitimate concerns. Either way, she didn't think it was a good time to tell Kate about her experience when reading the book. She thought it best not to mention anything about the book at all.

"Well, I think we're both crazy, and that's why we get along so well. I get why your parents wanted to keep you out of the loop with that book. But none of this changes our friendship," Brighton said.

"Yeah. Crazy. You can say that I guess," Kate said. She bit her bottom lip, staring at the window.

Chapter Eighteen
Tap, Tap, Tap

Brighton planned on falling asleep early. It was only two weeks until Halloween, and every movie she looked for on-demand involved something supernatural, gory, or flat-out scary. She loved this season and all of the thrills that accompanied it. The fact that her mom was working late tonight and the events of the last few days made her think a romantic comedy would be a wiser choice. As she scrolled through the guide, she heard a faint tapping. It must have been the heat turning on. The old furnace was known to create a series of rattles and bangs when the pipes started expanding. But she heard it again, tap, tap, tap. She muted the television and listened. It sounded like it was coming from upstairs.

She turned the volume back on, resumed searching for something to watch on the guide, and found a whimsical movie on the Hallmark Channel. Brighton concentrated on the storyline that, of course, involved charming characters and a predictable ending. It was perfect.

Tap, tap, tap. The sound continued. It could have been the heat, warming the radiators and making the crisp fall night cozy as she relaxed on the couch. There were several trees near the side of their house. Many of the branches needed pruning, so it was possible they now extended near the siding, slowly brushing against the exterior, tapping with each wind gust.

Brighton went into the kitchen, grabbed a raspberry iced tea and pretzels. She settled back onto the couch, checking her phone for any messages. She still had at least an hour until her mother got home, and it was too early to go to sleep.

Brighton knew she had seen this movie before, and she watched as the new girl in town quickly found true love, after bumping into him at the grocery store. He accidentally knocked into her, she dropped her groceries, and the rest was history. If only life played out that perfectly and that romantically. *Tap, tap, tap.* She turned up the volume but couldn't ignore the sound. It wasn't getting louder or more persistent, but it wasn't going away. She walked to the front door to make sure the doors were locked, while the persistent tapping continued. She had to find what was making that noise, and it sounded louder as she climbed the stairs.

With every footstep, the worn wood groaned. She wondered if the steps were always this noisy, or that she just never paid attention as she ran up and down them a million times. As she neared the top of the staircase, an all too familiar icy draft made her stop in her tracks. The door to her room was slightly ajar, and that's when she saw it. Faint patterns and shadows danced on the wooden floor in the hallway, spilling from her room. She pushed the door and realized that her strings of lights were twinkling. There was a strand in the corner that seemed to have come undone, the wires draped against her mirror. She walked over and held the small bulbs in her hand. The curtain lashed into the room, the open window allowing the sharp fall air to pour in. The wind howled outside, confirming the earlier forecast of predicted wind speeds up to forty-five mph gusts. As she dropped the strand of lights from her hand, she watched as it continued to sway. She moved across the room and sat on her bed, noticing the faded curtain panels stirring wildly in her bedroom. The light strand gently moved, tapping against the mirror.

She walked over to the window, put her hands on the edge, and leaned over to slam it shut. Darkness had already fallen since the days were getting shorter. She looked at the weapons, decapitated heads and blood-stained sheets hanging from the trees outside. Her neighbors went overboard when decorating for Halloween, going the route of slasher film rather than festive pumpkins. No wonder some of the neighborhood kids were hesitant to approach that porch on Halloween. The strobe light made Brighton's head hurt. She made sure to close the window tightly, as well as the blinds and curtains. The wind had to have been the culprit causing the tapping. She couldn't find any other cause.

The slamming door announced her mom's return. Late again. "Hello, I'm home," she heard her mom yell from downstairs.

She raced down the steps, as opposed to her cautious approach earlier.

"Hey, you're home," Brighton said, slightly out of breath. "What's for dinner?"

Her mom started taking groceries out of the bag. She looked at Brighton cautiously. "Are you okay? Why were you flying down the steps?"

"No reason. I'm happy you're home. I was watching a scary movie, and I guess I creeped myself out."

"Well, it is almost Halloween, so I guess that's the thing to do. I saw the neighbor's house. Don't you think it is a little over the top? I'm all for scary decorations, but the hanging body parts? That's a bit much, don't you think?"

"Yep. I'm not too surprised. That family acts strange year round. I *do* think it will scare some of the trick or treaters away. Hey, I wanted to ask you, were you doing anything to my room at all before you left for work?" she asked.

Her mom paused for a second and then continued folding grocery bags. "What do you mean by doing anything? I was in there grabbing laundry, but that's about it. Why do you ask? Are you looking for something?"

"My lights weren't working, but now they are. It seems like one of the strands fell, so maybe that was it. It's no big deal. But it was chilly when I came home. Do you remember opening the window?"

Her mom put down her fork and rested her hands on the table. "No, I'm not snooping around your room if that's what you're asking. You did need some fresh air circulating, though. Anyway, how is your study group going?"

"Study group is fine. Sorry, mom. I didn't mean you were snooping around. I think I need to get some sleep. All of these projects I am working on are getting to me. I have a lot going on."

As her mom started clearing the table, she leaned over and kissed her on the forehead.

"No one said high school was easy. You'll get through it. How about we both take a break and watch a movie? I think *The Shining* is available on-demand. That's a good scary movie for the season, but not over the top gory like our neighbors next door. Let me answer a few emails, and then I'll make some popcorn, okay?"

Brighton didn't have the heart to tell her *The Shining* was one of the last movies she wanted to watch. As she sat on the couch waiting for her mom to start the show, she listened for the tapping sound. It was gone.

It had to be the lights. Her mom was probably the one who opened the window, shifting the string of lights, and maybe kicking the book under the bed. She would have to look for it later but leaving it lost sounded like a better idea.

Before things got too crazy at the Overlook Hotel, Brighton told her mom she was too tired to finish the rest of the movie.

"Okay. We can finish it tomorrow. I'm going to watch the news then pack it in for the night. Good night, hon."

As she slowly pushed open her door, white lights illuminated the room. There was no breeze and no tapping. She lay on her bed and turned on one of the Hallmark movies to help her fall asleep.

CHAPTER NINETEEN
WITCHES IN BRADERTOWN

Brighton realized she slept longer than she wanted to even though it was Saturday. She promised Kate they would get together today. She reached for her phone and realized she had a lot of missed calls from her. The texts said she needed to help at her dad's shop today, but Brighton was welcome to come over and hang out. Brighton didn't have any other plans, and since her mom needed to go into the office for a few hours, she preferred doing anything else instead of staying home alone. She told her mom she'd get ready quickly, but she lingered under the hot shower, inhaling the scent of rosemary and mint shampoo. The warm water felt soothing on her face, and the steam lifted the fogginess of her slumber.

"Are you ready Brighton?" her mom yelled. "I can drop you off, but we have to leave soon."

As they pulled up to The Book Cellar, Kate was standing by the front door with a set of keys. It was still early, and she needed to open up for the day. As Brighton got out of the car, Kate greeted her with a huge smile.

"Hey, glad you're here early. You can help me open," Kate said while struggling with the keys. The door glided inward after Kate gave it a shove with her shoulder. "Come on inside."

The store was frigid, and the endless rows of books were obscured in darkness, tucked away in recesses of the shelves. Kate disappeared, and Brighton heard the rapid succession of snapping sounds. Within seconds, all of the sconces and overhead lights illuminated, and the store transformed into the inviting atmosphere she remembered from the other night.

"I'll put some coffee on and grab the cash drawer for the register. It's in the safe. Can you wait here in case anyone comes into the store? I'll be right out.

Kate disappeared into the back room without waiting for a response. Brighton walked to the front door and flipped the open sign. As she turned to walk back to the counter, she was startled by the sound of the door slamming.

"Hi! Glad you are open so early. Just wondering if you still have copies of the book?" a man said, taking off his hat and tucking it into his jacket. Without even questioning, she knew which book he was referring to.

"Well, this is a bookstore, we have tons of books," she joked.

"Come on. You know what I mean. The *possessed* book? I was here last week, and they were sold out. I'm hoping they got some. I heard there was a second place selling a few copies, but I couldn't track that place down," he said.

"Orwin's shop? I mean the Antique and Curiosities store. I believe that was a limited giveaway," she said.

"No, someone said there was another store selling them. Only a few copies though. I could be wrong. So, anyway, do you have any copies?"

"Let me check with the owner, I mean the owner's daughter. I was helping her open up this morning."

Just as she was about to walk into the backroom, Kate appeared, almost knocking Brighton over as she pushed through the swinging door. She held a small cardboard box that had a few layers of tape across the top.

"Hey, I'm looking for copies of the book. Have any?" the man said impatiently.

"Right here," Kate said, motioning to the box in her hands. "Bright, can you get me a box cutter or scissors? There should be something on the desk."

As Brighton located scissors neatly stored behind the desk, Kate began taking out the books. There only seemed to be fifteen copies or so. She didn't put them on the shelf but instead stacked them next to the register.

"Nice. I only need one copy. That's all it takes, right?" the man laughed.

"I'm not sure what you are talking about," Kate said while getting change out of the register. She didn't lift her head to look at the man, and Brighton knew Kate was fully aware of his reference.

"Come on. The curse or whatever it is. You know people died after reading the book, right?"

"I kind of heard something strange about the book. I think it's just a coincidence. But, hey, we will keep selling if people keep buying," she said, handing the man his change and a bag.

Brighton knew the customer was fishing for any information Kate knew about the book. Once the man completed the purchase, he turned to walk out of the store.

"Hey," Brighton yelled before he reached the door. He spun around, and Brighton could already see he had his phone to his ear. "If you think something bad could happen, why do you want the book anyway?"

The man stopped for a second and stared at the bag as if he never thought about it. "Everyone wants a copy. I guess I want to check it out and see what the hype is all about."

He crumpled the top of the bag and placed his hand on the door. The quizzical expression on his face proved Brighton's questioning made him uncomfortable. She wondered if he regretted his purchase. Before he exited the store, he stared at the bag in his hand and turned to look at Brighton.

"You know, it's like watching a scary movie or

going to a haunted house. The thrill of feeling fear and then the satisfaction of knowing you made it through, I guess," he said heading out the door. The satisfaction of scoring a copy of the book replaced the brief moment of concern. His phone was glued to his ear the minute the door shut behind him.

Kate stood in the corner laughing. "Well, you can tell you rattled him for a second at least. Why did you ask him that?"

"I don't know. I'm just trying to get an outsider's perspective."

She and Kate stared at the stacks of books neatly stacked in front of them knowing very well the entire town had the same perspective.

"Where did that box come from? It was weird the first customer was looking for the book, and you walked in with the box," Brighton said, breaking the silence.

"Well, that's what I was doing. Getting the cash drawer out of the safe and checking to see if we had any deliveries."

Brighton looked at the plain cardboard box. There were no shipping labels attached to the flap and no paper inserts inside.

"How was this delivered?" she said as she inspected the box in her hands.

"I guess you can say that it doesn't ship traditionally. Our guy drops them off when he has them available."

"Oh, the weird guy. I'd like to meet him."

"Here, come with me," Kate said as she headed to the rear of the store. Once outside, she stooped down and lifted the lid on a silver box placed next to the door. "Recently, *he* contacted my dad and told him he had a shipment. My dad left a check under the box behind the store, and then our guy left the books there. Check gone, books here, and Dad sells them." Kate wiped her hands on her pants and secured the door behind her. "Easy peasy."

"Aren't you afraid someone is going to take them? A box of the most sought after book lying around outside?" Brighton asked.

Kate kicked the metal container, and it didn't move. "It's bolted to the side of the building. My dad leaves it open, but there's a lock on it. Once the delivery is placed inside, the lid is closed and it locks. Only my dad can open it. Also, this small compartment inside allows my dad to conceal the envelope with the check. Nothing to see, nothing to steal."

Satisfied with the secret drop-off setup, Brighton followed Kate back into the store.

"I guess your dad stopped toying with the idea of not carrying the books anymore? I know he was worried about the negative stories surrounding it, but any press is good press."

Kate didn't say much and turned to count some of the bills in the drawer. "Who knows what he will do. All I know is the box was there this morning, and the check was gone. The timing was great. Interested in the coffee I just brewed? If not, my mom has different kinds of K-Cups stashed in the back. I think she has apple cider and hot chocolate."

"Hot chocolate is fine, thanks."

Kate disappeared again, and Brighton heard the trickling of water, meaning she must have found the hot chocolate. The store looked different during the day. The sun streaming through the windows made it lose some of its evening coziness, but it was still pleasant. Brighton thought some oversized chairs and couches would add to the ambiance, but Kate explained that due to the small space, they wanted to keep their customers moving rather than lingering with their purchase. That is also the reason they decided against selling coffee and snacks. It made sense.

As Brighton walked around scanning the titles of books, she noticed a small, round table in the corner, with a handwritten sign that read "LOCAL" in bold black letters. As she leafed through some of the pages, various local authors penned stories and history about the railroad industry, coal mining, and other pertinent facts connected to their region.

One of the books on the back of the table caught

her eye. The glossy cover was cobalt blue and covered with wispy, ghost-like images. There weren't many pages, but the table of contents reflected material as expected from the title of the book *Supernatural and Unexplained Bradertown*.

Brighton paged through the tales of sightings of ghostly figures that appeared late at night in the middle of the road, and houses that had documented events ranging from everything from flying objects to strange apparitions and voices. Although not necessarily supernatural, circumstances surrounding widely publicized crimes were included in the book. Usually, when there was a famous story of murder or violent crime, it is accompanied by a blurb explaining that others experienced unusual events at the locations where these crimes took place. None of these stories were too surprising; she had heard most of them before, or at least different variations. One could probably insert any city name into the title of the book, and residents would identify with a story that fit the details. Every town was built on legend and folklore that was passed down through generations. As she was about to return the book to the table, she flipped past something that didn't sound familiar. The title of the chapter was "Modern Day Witch Hunt."

"That's a neat book, isn't it?" Kate appeared holding a steaming cup of cocoa. "Here, all I could find was chocolate mint. It smells good," she said, shrugging and handing the Styrofoam cup to Brighton.

The aroma of chocolate and peppermint swirled under her nose, but the rising steam told her it was too hot to drink. She picked up the book, showing the cover to Kate.

"This is pretty interesting. I heard most of these stories over the years, but I was about to read the section about witches."

"Can I see that for a second?"

Kate reached over to grab it as Brighton handed it to her. "I read this recently, and I was going to ask you about that. Do you remember hearing stories about witchcraft? While a lot of the stories cover a large northeast region, not all of them are about local history—but this one is."

Brighton didn't recall ever hearing anything about witchcraft. She remembered her mom saying that back in the '90s everyone was afraid their kids were going to be kidnapped and sacrificed due to a story circulating about an increase of devil worship in the area. It turned out it was a group of teenagers drawing some symbols on abandoned buildings and leaving ritual paraphernalia behind. It was a prime example of how one bit of information became greatly exaggerated.

Every now and again the story resurfaces about the time the town feared the crazy devil worshippers, and every time someone sets the record straight about what really happened. Those incidents weren't even included in this book. But there was a chapter on witches.

"I never heard any stories about witchcraft in this area. Are you sure it was referring to this region?" Brighton asked.

"It says right here," Kate said, reading from the book, "While there has never been a public arena in recent decades where someone was accused of witchcraft, the power of persuasion, relentless gossip and the fear of the unusual and the unknown could be just as accusatory. A woman named Lorna was well known in the town for creating her homeopathic medicines and herbs. In the early days, friends and neighbors would turn to her in the hopes of curing their ailments. As the onset of modern medicine became more popular, synthetically-created drugs were a more coveted answer to treat the public's general malaise. Lorna's source of income to help support her family came from selling her herbs, handmade clothing, and other trinkets that she crafted. She had a young daughter who passed away from unknown causes.

Rumors started that Lorna tried to treat her daughter with her "witch potions" and was negligent in taking her for proper medical care. When Lorna's husband passed away a few months later, the gossip in the town overwhelmingly pointed to the fact that it couldn't be sheer coincidence that both her daughter and husband died so suddenly. Lorna became a recluse, and not much more was known about her. She never came out of her house, let alone sell anything to anyone. People say that after the loss of her daughter and husband plus the fact that she couldn't turn to her friends and neighbors for help, she went insane. Those that did see her leave her home on a rare occasion would see her wandering around, talking to herself, rambling on about evil spirits and their return."

Kate closed the book and held it close to her chest.

"It's kind of sad. I think putting this story in the category of witchcraft is a bit of a stretch. I think it's more about a woman who lost everything and everyone around her and went insane.

"Kate, what time is your dad getting here?"

"He said he would be here by lunchtime, why?"

"We need to go back to your house. I have to show you something."

CHAPTER TWENTY
BIKE RIDES AND BIRDHOUSES

After grabbing a sandwich at Kate's house, Brighton told her they needed to go for a walk. She wanted to explain the entire situation to her, but she thought it was easier to show her evidence to support her theories. As they entered the cemetery, decayed leaves scattered in a frenzy like burnt embers from a fire. Brighton rubbed her hands together, cupping them to her face, exhaling and hoping to warm her frozen fingers as Kate tried to keep up with her.

"Are we going to your house?" Kate asked.

"Trust me. I need to show you something."

Brighton slowed her pace as she searched for the same spot she was in just the other day. The sun wasn't hitting the other headstone in the exact place, and she couldn't use that as a guide to the same area. The tall grass gently brushed her hand as they weaved in and out of the rows of graves. Brighton became frustrated as she scoured the names, and she could tell Kate was also becoming irritated.

"Bright, what are you looking for?" Kate asked, stooping down to read one of the inscriptions.

Finally, she saw it. The small, white lamb was in clear view, perched atop the stone, watching over all the graves. Her heart sank, after finding out from her research that years ago many children's graves were marked with a small white angel or lamb to signify the innocence lost at such a young age. Kate followed her as they made their way through the sea of overgrown weeds. The cemetery looked maintained from the first appearance, but as they moved farther in, the graves were not as well kept as the outer rows closer to the road.

"Kate, look. This is what I was talking about before, remember? Look at the names." Brighton stood back, arms crossed, waiting for Kate to see the revelation.

"Okay. It looks like a husband, wife, and daughter are buried here." Kate crouched down, teetering on the tips of her black sneakers with pink laces dragging on the ground. "Abner, Lorna, and beloved daughter," she said, slowly dragging her finger over the inscription.

Brighton sighed, and the snapping twigs sounded like kindling crackling in a fireplace as she walked over to move closer to the stone. She placed her finger on the inscription. "Look at the names. The last name is Karender. But look at this one, Lorna Rellim Karender." She stepped back waiting for a look of shock on Kate's face.

Kate stared at the names in front of her. "And? I guess I'm missing it," she said, turning to Brighton. The expression on her face was as if she just bit into a lemon.

"Kate. Lorna Rellim Karender? This is what I was saying the other day. Rellim. The author of *My Skull Possession*?" she said, hoping this would ring a bell.

"I get it. It's the same last name. But why would that mean she was the author of the book? It could have been a common last name in the town years ago, or maybe a distant relative. But it's Lorna Rellim Karender. That's not even the correct first name. I know it seems like a strange coincidence, but I think that's all it is."

Brighton was growing more frustrated by the minute. How could Kate not think this was bizarre? After reading the story about the woman accused of witchcraft and realizing that the same name is on *My Skull Possession*, how could she not see the connection?

Brighton took a picture of the stone and slid her phone back into her pocket. As they began to walk back to the path, she tried to piece all of the information together that was swirling around in her head. She remembered Kate's dad explained to her that the person who drops the books off is a distant relative of the original author.

"When my mom and I stopped by the store, your dad explained that the person he gets the books from is self-published, and they have some connection to the author." She waited for Kate to interject as they neared her house.

"Right," she said, pausing on the front porch. "But, Bright, authors use pen names all the time. Also, and humor me for a second, what if we weren't the only ones who happened to read the book of local folklore. Imagine if someone took that information and used it to their advantage. The tragic story of Lorna could be connected to any book."

Brighton understood what she was saying. She also recognized how coincidental it was the book about Bradertown just happened to be on the table today. There were too many coincidences surrounding the situation, and Brighton wanted to find out why.

"Okay, I have to admit when I first heard about this book, I was skeptical about the rumors that were circulating. But I feel like I need to know more about Lorna Rellim Karender. I need to find out why I am the only one stumbling upon these connections. Don't you think we should at least ask Orwin what he knows about the name or some of the town's history?" Brighton pleaded.

"You should really look into pursuing a career as an investigator," Kate said. She hesitated before continuing. "Okay, so what is your plan?"

"I think we need to talk to Orwin. We also need to see if your dad could find out more about his contact person for the book."

"I don't know. I told you my parent's stance on this. If I go snooping around looking for answers to explain the mystery around this book, they aren't going to be too happy."

Brighton only wanted to find out more information about the person distributing the books.

"Kate, do you have access to your dad's contact numbers?"

"I don't. But, before we left the store, I told my dad we got fifteen copies today. He said that was only half of what he was promised. My dad called, and his guy said he would drop off the rest tomorrow morning."

Brighton knew this was their chance to try to find out a little more about their mystery book salesman. "Do you know what time he is coming? Tell your dad you'll stay at the store tomorrow morning, too."

"I guess that could work. Let me talk to my dad and see what I can do.

With that, Brighton knew Kate was on board. Not only did Kate convince her dad to let her work at the store in the morning, but she found out the timing of the book delivery. Brighton was hopeful that meeting the only person with a connection to the author of *My Skull Possession* would provide insight into the history of the book.

"I am assuming you are going to be here bright and early tomorrow morning, too," Kate said. "It's probably a good idea, since the guy might be a total creep. I'd rather have you around.

The next morning, Brighton told her mom she was helping Kate and needed to be dropped off at the store around 7:30 a.m. She peered through the window but didn't see any signs of Kate in the darkened store. Brighton was about to call her when she heard scuffling near the door.

"Sorry, I just got here myself. We haven't had a delivery yet, but it is expected around 8 a.m.," Kate said, letting Brighton in.

Brighton zipped her coat, thrusting her hands deep into the pockets. The Book Cellar looked inviting as usual, but it felt like the recesses of the store's namesake.

"Listen, I'll stay out of the way. It might be weird if he sees two people here so early waiting for a small shipment of books."

As she was explaining the game plan to Kate, they both watched as a shadow passed by the frosted glass window. Brighton ran over to the door and crouched down beside it. She heard a thump and motioned to Kate to look out the door and see who it was. Kate slowly pushed the gathered curtain away from the small window.

"Looks like our guy is early," Kate whispered as

she strained to peer out the window. "And, he is leaving a box at the door. He's leaving on a bike!" she said with surprise.

"What do you mean a bike? A motorcycle?" Brighton asked.

"No, like a bicycle bike. I guess that's why the deliveries aren't huge, and he stops by often."

Kate's body was pressed against the door as she stood on her tiptoes. If this delivery guy happened to look through the door and see her peeking out the window and Brighton crouched on the floor, she wouldn't blame him if he thought something was amiss.

"Ugh. If I had my bike, I would follow him. There is no way I can keep up even if I tried to run," Brighton said.

Kate quickly turned to Brighton. "Come on, hurry," she said, running to the back storeroom. Boxes tumbled, and Brighton tripped on a mop and bucket.

"My dad keeps a mountain bike in here. He always says he wants to get some exercise on his lunch and explore the town, but you know how that goes. Here. Go, go, go, before he leaves."

The two of them carefully inched their way through the storeroom and led the bike right through the front of the store. Brighton steadied the knobby rubber handlebars as Kate unlocked the door. They waited until they saw a man with a black hoodie exit from the alley next to the store. Brighton patted her pocket to make sure she had her phone. The pedal dug into her shin as she rushed to take the bike out of the store.

"Be careful," Kate said.

Brighton pedaled as fast as she could to catch up with the hooded rider. A brisk morning bike chase was not something she expected. Brighton planned on trailing him at a considerable distance, but she didn't want to lose him. The morning fog started to lift, but the cold wind stung her face as she raced through the streets. She kept her target in view but allowed a couple of blocks in between, so she would not be spotted. Brighton was sure the man had no reason to think anyone was following him. He wasn't even aware she was anywhere near the vicinity of the store when he dropped the books off.

As they neared a less populated area of town, Brighton wondered how much farther she should follow. He turned near one of the many cemeteries in town and cycled up the hill. Brighton hoped he was concentrating on making it up the incline and not who was behind him. Her lungs were on fire while her face felt frozen. She pushed with all of her energy to reach the top of the hill and struggled to catch her breath once she did. Brighton moved the bike closer to the tree line as cars whisked by her as they crested the hill and followed the curve of the road. From her position, she could see the hooded biker coasting to the bottom.

"There you are," she said out loud.

Dust swirled up at the beginning of the dirt road, and Brighton saw him weave his way along the less traveled route. She knew there was a farm near the end of the road, as well as a few small homes. Near the end of the row of houses, there was a path that many bikers and joggers took. If Brighton road the bike into that area, it was not uncommon to follow the trail as many other hikers and cyclists did. Traveling through the tree covered forest path alone wasn't something she welcomed on this frosty morning, but it would work if it meant not blowing her cover. She could quickly take this path without seeming suspicious.

The brakes squealed as she tightly gripped the levers on the handlebars, cringing every time a car drove by as each passing vehicle seemed to inch dangerously close. As she neared the turn, the man was no longer in sight.

Gravel kicked up around her and pelted the tops of her feet as she came to an abrupt stop. The fork in the road prompted her to decide—should she investigate the farm area on the left or the cluster of houses on the right? As she veered to the right, the road became narrower. She pulled over into the tall grass on the side and waited for a truck to pass. The rocks crunched under the bicycle tires as she picked up momentum. The next house was a well-kept mobile home. There was no car in the driveway, but Brighton could see a woman standing in the kitchen. She assumed the truck that drove by before pulled away from this quaint homestead. The woman looked up from whatever she was doing and noticed Brighton.

"Hi," Brighton yelled and waved as she passed by. At least someone knew she was here.

There was no sign of the man on the bike. It was possible he traveled over to the farm, but Brighton didn't think that was where he lived. She kept her bike close to the side of the road near the line of trees as she tried to plot her next move. There was only one bar on her phone, and Brighton wasn't sure how strong the signal would be farther into her journey.

Just as she was about to get back on the road, she heard a sound like someone slowly snapping a piece of plywood.

"Hello?" she said. The woods responded with a louder crackling, like a burning log settling in a fireplace. Brighton jumped off the bike and let it fall to the ground. Just as she landed near the road, a large branch came crashing down, becoming entwined in the handlebars. She walked over to make sure there wasn't any damage, and the smooth sole of her shoe glided across a small patch of mud like an ice skate. Her hands broke her fall, but not before she received a deep gash across her palm. Brighton felt as if she touched a hot iron, and looked down to see a trickle of crimson running down her hand. She searched her pocket, hoping she still had tissues stashed in the zipper compartment of her jacket. She fished them out, pressing the folded square against her hand. The cut wasn't as severe as initially thought, but it stung. She reached for the hair tie that kept her long strands away from her face. The black elastic band fit perfectly around her palm and kept the tissues in place.

"That should work for now," she said while brushing off her pants and picking up the mountain bike. Brighton was relieved there was no damage but wondered what could have caused the limb to fall. Could it have been the recent rain weakening the trees? Before any other unfortunate luck accompanied her on this journey, she decided to head back. The man was long gone, and she felt foolish setting out on this chase anyway. Just as she was walking her bike, she could see something in the distance. A faint trace of white smoke climbed through barren trees. It looked like it wasn't very far away, but it wasn't on the same road as the other houses she had passed. As she inched forward, she could make out a small stack from where the smoke originated.

Brighton shook her hand, hoping the throbbing would stop soon. The tissue was marred by a splash of deep red that seeped through the wrinkled whiteness.

She shifted her weight to one handlebar and was satisfied that the wound stopped bleeding for now. After a rigorous and exhausting ride to get here, she knew she might as well continue and check out the last house in view. Brighton kept to the side of the road, but not too close to any of the trees, hoping to avoid any additional injuries. The small house was barely visible from the street, but Brighton could see it wasn't far as she turned onto the short driveway. She carefully leaned her bike against a tree and made her way closer to get a better view.

Every twig and leaf that snapped and crunched echoed as if she was standing at the base of a cavern. A looming maple tree served as an excellent hiding point, and Brighton leaned against the massive trunk. She could see the modest white trailer. The windows were dark, except for one filled with a hazy straw yellow. A green canopy disrupted the clean lines of the home, shading the brick steps leading to the entrance.

As Brighton approached the trailer, she was surprised at how well maintained it was. The chocolate mulch deeply contrasted against the starch white siding. The air filled with the smell of burning wood. Meticulous rows of shrubs created a naturally defined property line. Brighton wasn't sure what kind of bushes they were, but it looked like something that may have once bloomed in season. A small storage shed sat in the far corner of the property.

Screech. Slam.

Brighton imagined a strand of thread tugging at her scalp, forcing her to stand as straight as possible. She could feel the indentations forming on her skin as her body became one with the bark. She prayed whoever it was didn't see her as she tried to dissolve into the background of the forest. The slow rustling of leaves was interrupted by the sound of something surging through the brush. Groaning hinges made Brighton want to peer around the tree to see who went into the house. Or if someone else came out. She inched forward just enough to catch a glimpse of a man in a faded, black hoodie, his long chalky gray hair tightly gathered at the base of his neck. Brighton was sure he could hear the hammering of her heart.

Slam!

Brighton folded over, her elbows resting on her knees. Wetness oozed down her hand and dotted the ground with specks of red. The remnants of the bloody makeshift bandage fell from her palm like shriveled petals. She knew she needed to get back soon but needed to confirm she wouldn't be seen. Brighton waited for what seemed like hours, but in reality, only ten minutes had passed before she moved a muscle.

She plotted each step, avoiding anything that would crunch or snap. She found the handlebars and guided the bike to the driveway. As her confidence returned and breathing regulated, she stopped to study the compact dwelling. There were rows of shrubs behind the home, as well as additional storage units. They were tall, boxy, and aligned with the precision of an architect.

"Maybe birdhouses," she thought.

The balance and well-maintained landscape seemed peculiar. Not that it wasn't appealing, but it stood in great contrast to the man living inside. As the tendrils of smoke cascaded up to meet barren branches reaching to the clouded sky, Brighton took a few pictures before heading home.

CHAPTER TWENTY-ONE
SORRY, WE'RE CLOSED

"We might have a medical kit in the back, hang on," Kate said as she rummaged in the storeroom at the bookshop.

Brighton felt like she would collapse. The gaping wound stung as Kate squeezed a cotton ball saturated with peroxide over it.

"I don't think it needs stitches," Kate said as she applied a bandage.

Brighton flexed her fingers and made a fist. It felt tight but was more annoying than anything. She knew it would be hard to heal since it was in the crease of her hand.

"So that branch just fell? Did you hit it with the bike or anything?" Kate asked, cleaning up the medical kit.

"No. I was close to the side of the road where the wooded area started, but I didn't touch any of the trees. It had to be from the storm the other day."

"I guess," Kate said, raising her eyebrows.

Brighton knew it was odd that it happened the way that it did, but she tried not to dwell on it. She was happy that her hand was the only injury she sustained.

"I guess what I am wondering is, what exactly did you find out?" she asked.

Brighton wasn't sure what she found out; she didn't even know what she was looking for. All she knew was that their bookseller rode a bike, lived in a tidy little white house in the middle of the woods, and didn't seem very social. Unconventional, yes, but not extraordinarily bizarre or concerning.

"Maybe we'll have better luck talking to Orwin," Kate said. "My dad should be back soon. Maybe I'll call my mom, and she can give us a ride over. Is he open now?" Brighton checked her phone and was pleased to see in the website description it was green, meaning he was open. "We're good. He's open."

As Kate's mom drove them to the store, she asked how long they planned on staying. "Maybe I can hang out at that little coffee shop where you meet with your study group," she said. As they pulled up in front of the store, Kate told her mom not to leave yet.

"Hold on, Mom," Kate said, alarmed.

"Bright, I don't think it's open," she said, peering out the window. The storefront was dark, but there was a white paper taped to the door.

Brighton jumped out of the back seat and read the note fluttering on the glass door.

"What does it say?" Kate yelled out the window.

"Closed due to an emergency," Brighton read out

loud. She peered in the window looking for any explanation as to why Orwin's store remained closed, especially since weekends were probably busy. She assumed it could be anything from electrical problems to a death or illness in the family. Brighton didn't recall Orwin mentioning any close family members, but neither of them delved into any stories about their personal lives. Brighton slid back into the car, with Kate turned around from the front waiting for an explanation.

"I don't know. There's just that note. I guess something happened," Brighton said, watching the store disappear as Kate's mom pulled away.

"Yeah, something must have happened," Kate said. Her usual, boisterous voice was barely a mumble. Brighton knew Kate felt the same way as she did. Something wasn't right.

They pulled in front of Kate's house.

"You know, I need to run to the store. Do you girls want to go with me?" Joelle asked.

"No, we will stay here. See you in a bit," Kate said, getting out of the car.

Brighton welcomed the opportunity to have some time to discuss the situation as they hurried into the house. Kate grabbed a bag of salt and vinegar chips, dumping it into a bowl between the two of them. Brighton didn't even look up from her phone.

"I know we don't know a lot about him, but

something doesn't seem right. I don't recall anyone else working at the store, do you? Who would have put that sign there?" Kate said while licking salt from her fingers.

Brighton scrolled through Orwin's Facebook page, looking for any indication of what may have happened. A few comments were asking about store hours. About ten comments down, she saw a post that grabbed her attention.

"Kate, look at this. Someone posted that they heard Orwin collapsed and was rushed to the hospital." She grabbed the phone and started reading the comments. As she handed the phone back, her face lost its color.

"Looks like the rumors are starting already. Someone commented Orwin was almost the next victim," she said.

"What does that mean?"

"Bright, you know what it means. Orwin gets copies of *My Skull Possession*, and this happens. You start reading it and look what happened to you," she said, motioning to Brighton's wrapped hand. "There might be something to this after all," Kate's voice quivered. She drew her long legs in front of her and pulled her sweatshirt over her knees. She rested her face, obscuring her mouth and nose. "It's not good. It's not good, Bright. It's just like last time," she said putting her head down.

Brighton knew Kate was thinking about everything that happened in the past. She could understand how that could happen. All of the cases Kate talked about had a long history attached to it, and many also carried unexplained supernatural stories as well. But there were a lot of assumptions here, and Brighton knew they needed to get more information before *My Skull Possession* became the next famous object ghost hunters sought.

"Hey, relax," she said, putting her arm around Kate's shoulders. "We'll get to the bottom of this. It's fine," she said. "Let's check with your dad to see what he knows about Orwin. Maybe he talked to him when he sold him the books."

Brighton was unnerved as she started to string together some of the events that occurred in the last few days surrounding the book, but right now she was concerned with what happened to Orwin.

"I can't ask my dad. He won't know," she said, still resting her head on her knees. Her voice was muffled, her hair cascading down to her feet.

"Well, it can't hurt to ask. Maybe Orwin mentioned something about family members, or…"

"He didn't sell him the books," she whispered, still projecting her voice down to the floor.

"He what?" Brighton said.

"My dad never sold any books to Orwin," she said, stretching her hands out in front of her. As she straightened her back and pushed her hands against her bed, she stared at the ceiling. "When we moved here, my parents hoped it was the right choice. The bookstore seemed to take off from the beginning, and my dad normally didn't gamble on carrying books like *My Skull Possession*. I told you if he couldn't return unsold copies, he didn't carry it. But this guy was adamant. He told my dad he tried several places to carry his books, but none would agree. I guess my dad felt sorry for him and agreed to a small shipment. He promised our store would be the only outlet to carry them, and when it became popular, it would be The Book Cellar only that would profit."

Brighton took a second to absorb what Kate was telling her. "Is it possible that someone other than Orwin bought several copies and gave them to Orwin for his shop?"

"I don't know. I guess it is possible. But listen. My dad doesn't want this. We don't want this. We don't want to be known as the only bookstore where you can get a book that causes the readers to die. My dad said this week is it."

"No more deliveries?"

"That's what he said."

"We need to talk to Orwin and find out where he got those books. And, more importantly, find out if he is okay," Brighton said. Kate nodded but was apparently in a different place.

When Brighton returned home, she immediately

retreated to her room. Her mom's footsteps were not far behind.

"Could I come in for a second?" she said, standing in the doorway.

"Sure," Brighton said, hoping she wouldn't ask about her wounded hand.

"Hey, I just wanted to make sure everything is okay," she said, smoothing the down-filled comforter.

"I'm fine. Just a long week." Her mom walked over to her closet, slid the door open and reached the top shelf.

"Is it because of this?" she said, waving a copy of *My Skull Possession* in the air.

"Why is that there?" Brighton said as she jumped up to grab the book.

"It was under your bed. When did you start reading it?"

Brighton wondered how she knew she was reading it. Without even answering, her mom continued.

"The last few nights, you've had a lot of trouble sleeping. Every time I heard a noise, I would check on you, and you were tossing and turning. I figured something was bothering you, and when I was doing a thorough cleaning of your room, I found it under your bed. Honey, don't read it if it bothers you that much. Plus, I wanted to ask how Kate is with all of this."

"What do you mean?"

"Look, I talked to Kate's mom when they first moved here. I knew you were spending a lot of time with her, so of course, when I ran into her parents, I made it a point to get to know them. Did she tell you about some of Kate's earlier struggles?"

"I know. Kate told me about it."

"Well, then you know after Kate was released from the facility, her parents vowed to keep her away from anything that could cause her to relapse. When you said you and Kate were talking about this book being connected to something supernatural and asking questions about all of these crazy things, I was a little concerned that maybe it was best you didn't spend as much time with Kate."

Her mom continued about how the Dorns wanted to make a fresh start here. They were happy when Kate did so well in school and found such a great friend. She lost Brighton at the mention of released from the facility, but she didn't want to let on she didn't know that part of the story. As her mom droned on, her mind raced with thoughts about this new piece of information. She pictured pretty Kate, her trendy clothes replaced with a hospital gown, her confidence diminished as she sat in therapy sharing her fears and anxieties. Trays of food brought in, medicine administered. Did she go willingly? Was she afraid to be alone at night? Brighton knew once the first tear broke free, she would have a hard time stopping the steady stream. She needed to be alone.

"Thanks for the concern, Mom, but Kate seems to be acting fine to me," Brighton said, trying to act as if her heart wasn't aching for her friend. "And I don't plan on reading any more of that book anyway."

Her mom closed the door, seeming satisfied with her response. Brighton pulled up Facebook to check for any updates on Orwin's page. There were hundreds of comments now, most of them speculative.

The book is haunted, Orwin made his last sale.

I heard the whole town is cursed.

Before she placed her phone on the dresser to charge, she noticed one last message updated with the time stamp, JUST NOW.

It read, *I heard Orwin is at Morris Memorial Hospital.*

Brighton texted Kate to let her know about the recent update and where they were going tomorrow. As she hit refresh, the message about Orwin disappeared. Someone deleted it as fast as it was posted. Brighton's finger hovered over her phone. She debated whether she should let Kate know the story her mom told her. Her stomach turned as she envisioned what Kate must have gone through.

She placed her phone face down and made sure the alarm was set. Brighton wasn't sure she could handle any more conversations about hospitals or institutions tonight. The plug from the Christmas lights dangled against the wall, the Super Blender infomercial blared from the television, and the bedside lamp kept away shadows as she tried to fall asleep.

CHAPTER TWENTY-TWO
MRS. JONESDOCHTER

At lunch, Kate loaded the Uber app on her phone. They both decided that asking for a ride to the hospital would send too many red flags. Kate used a prepaid card and agreed to all the terms. It was cheaper than a cab, more convenient than the bus—and didn't prompt any nagging questions from parents.

"I hope this works," Kate said while checking her email confirmation. "I think I did everything right. Let's meet one block down from the school as soon as last period is over."

The day seemed to drag on. Brighton was looking forward to seeing Orwin. She hoped he was okay but felt selfish she had many questions she needed him to answer. She tried to tell herself it wasn't incredibly unusual to hear someone like Orwin landed in the hospital. While he was a vibrant man who was full of energy, he wasn't exactly the picture of health. She tried to ignore the fact he became incapacitated not long after he came into possession of the books, but she couldn't remove that entirely from her mind. Brighton also thought it best not to bring up the fact of the additional details she found out about Kate's past. Although she shared her experience about the mirror and some other events in her travels, Kate never once brought up about being institutionalized.

The Uber driver arrived. It was the first time either of them had used the service, so they were a little nervous. Kate looked relieved when they saw an older woman pull up in a modest, compact car. Kate signaled for Brighton to come over, and they both got in.

"Morris Hospital, right, girls?" the cheerful woman said. It seemed as if their driver barely cleared the steering wheel to see over the dash, but with her seat pulled all the way up, she didn't have any problems as she pulled away from the curb.

"My name is Mrs. Jonesdochter. I know. It's a mouthful. You can call me Peg. I'll be your driver," she said, glancing up at the rearview mirror at Brighton. Kate sat in the front seat, giving Brighton her best "Isn't she just adorable?" shoulder shrug and smile.

"Hi Peg," Kate said. "Not a long drive today. Just over to the hospital to see a friend."

"Oh, I hope it's nothing serious," she said, raising her hand to her mouth. Her bracelets jangled as she returned her hand to the steering wheel.

"We shouldn't be long," Kate said, not offering too much more information. "Can we request you to take us back to school?"

"You sure can. All through the app. It's pretty neat if you ask me." She reached into her blue jacket, pulling out the equivalent of a box of tissues. After fishing in her pocket, she found something else and offered it to Kate. "Candy?"

Kate looked back at Brighton and gave her that charming smile again. "I'm good, Peg, but thanks. Here, Brighton, you take it," she said, handing her three brightly wrapped hard candies.

"Thanks." Brighton tucked them in her pocket.

"Well, the hospital is right up here. When you are ready, do your stuff on the phone, and I'll be back. I might go for some coffee. And then I'll take you back to school."

Morris Hospital wasn't a large medical center. They walked into the lobby, scanning the area, trying to find the patient rooms. A red glow spilled onto the glossy floor near the far left wall, alerting those looking for the emergency room. A small unoccupied desk sat at the back of the lobby with a phone in the center. Several green lights were flashing, but there was no indication of what the connections were.

"I guess we dial an operator," Kate said, picking up the slim, black handset and pushing the keypad. "Hi, we are looking for Orwin," she said, dragging out the last consonant. Kate placed her hand over the receiver, her brown eyes wide with alarm. "We don't even know his last name. Do we?" she whispered. Before Brighton could even answer her, Kate moved the phone back near her face and listened intently. "Thank you so much."

"What? They didn't ask?"

"I guess there is only one Orwin checked in. Room 232."

Brighton followed her to the elevator and moved to the side as a hospital worker wheeled someone in on a gurney. He positioned the mobile hospital bed in the middle of the elevator, separating Kate and Brighton. Kate stood in the corner, staring at the IV drip that was attached to the patient. She quickly looked down at the floor, biting her bottom lip. Her eyes darted from the IV bag to the floor, her defined eyebrows furrowed. Brighton wondered if she was thinking of her time spent in a hospital setting, or if she was uncomfortable sharing the same space with a patient uneasy as they were. The light flashed, and the quiet ding of the bell announced they were on their floor. Kate squeezed past the gurney and escort next to it. She seemed like she was in a hurry to get out. Brighton decided to ignore the entire situation altogether and instead changed the subject to Orwin.

"So, what room did they say? 232?" she said.

"Yes, it looks like it's down here," Kate said, staring at the sign indicating patient rooms with arrows and numbers.

As they made their way down the hall, several

nurses bustled around them, too busy to give them any direction. The smell of antiseptic floor cleaner and the daily lunch that was being distributed was not the most pleasant scent. She peered into one of the rooms as a woman removed a dark green cover from an arrangement of chicken and potatoes, with a side of peas and a small dinner roll. The chicken was covered with bright yellow gravy that oozed over the edge of the plate. As they moved to the next room, Brighton caught Kate staring with disapproval at the trays of hospital food.

"Doesn't look too appetizing, does it?" Brighton said.

"No, hospital food never is," Kate said without taking her eyes from the patient's lunch. "Let's find Orwin."

As they located the room number, the door wasn't open all the way. Kate peered in and knocked lightly. She pushed it open and motioned for Brighton to follow.

"Hello?" Kate said as they continued into the room. Her voice warbled like a bird, not matching her usual boisterous disposition. The blinds were drawn, and the overhead lights were off. The other side of the semi-private room was vacant, and Brighton could hear voices. As they moved closer to the bed, she realized the small TV in the corner was on with light dancing against the array of machines that occasionally beeped.

"Hi, please, come in," a male voice said. It didn't sound like Orwin, and Brighton quickly realized it didn't come from him. Lying in the bed was Orwin, hooked up to an IV and several monitors. The machines reflected that he was stable, but his eyes were closed. The cream-colored thermal blanket was pulled up to his chest, a mess of blue wires stretching across his arms and connected to the devices next to him. Violet crescents below his eyes disrupted the sallow pallor of his face.

"I'm Kate, and this is Brighton," she said to the young man who stood up next to the bed. "We're friends of Orwin's. I mean, we just met him at the shop a few weeks ago, and have been coming to the store. When we saw someone post he was in the hospital, we were concerned," she said, staring at Orwin. "Is he conscious?"

"Uh, in and out. I'm Brett. Orwin's nephew." Tall and thin, clad in a navy hooded jacket, faded baseball cap, and jeans, he looked the opposite of Orwin.

"What happened? Did he get sick?" Kate asked.

Brett looked over at his uncle, and without losing focus, he said, "You mean, did something happen to him out of the ordinary?"

"What? Oh, no, that's not what I meant," Kate said. Brighton knew all too well that it was definitely on her mind, also.

"It's fine. Most people inquiring about him ask the same thing. I'm used to it. My mom got the call he collapsed at the store. One of his customers found him on the floor near the back room. He had a very irregular heartbeat and was really out of it. He is weak and has been in and out of consciousness. They stabilized him, but he is going to be in here for a few days until he's out of the woods. My mom has always said he never took care of himself, so that's what got him here. And that's why I am here."

"Well, that's nice of you to sit with him. What do they think it is? Something with his heart?" Brighton asked, staring at the green glow from the monitors. She thought someone who was supposed to be close family sounded a bit harsh about the situation.

"They are still running tests, but they aren't sure. Orwin was breathing when they found him, but he was pretty sick. He vomited and had a fever. They think it could be a strain of flu that's going around. We have to wait and see. Lucky someone found him though. It's a good thing his store is always busy."

"We won't stay long. We just wanted to check in and see how Orwin is doing. I'm glad to hear he is stable," Kate said, moving back to the door.

"Oh, it looks like it's his heart rate again. I'm sure the nurses will be in," Brett said, staring at the screen. Two nurses appeared and ushered Kate and Brighton to the back of the room. They heard a low moan and saw his feet moving under the blanket.

"Let's go," Kate whispered.

"We'll get you some good stuff, don't worry," they heard Brett say. Kate looked at Brighton, confused.

"I'm sorry?" she said, poking her head back in the room.

"Oh, no. I was talking to my uncle. Now and then he becomes coherent and tries to talk. He just said coffee. I know the stuff here is pretty bad, so I told him I'd get him some good stuff when he is a little better." The nurse gave him an irritated look and wrote something on the clipboard.

"Well, that's more like Orwin, asking for coffee. Next time we see him, we'll have to remember to get him some *good stuff*," Brighton laughed.

"Yes! I finally have reception," Kate said as they went down to the lobby. "Let me get into the app, so we can bring Peg back."

While Kate concentrated on her phone, Brighton noticed the burgundy compact car across the street. "Kate, I think Peg is already waiting for us," Brighton said, walking back into the hospital.

They approached the car, and Peg leaned over to open the door. "I thought I would hang around here as I said. It works out better sometimes. How is your friend? Okay, I hope?"

"He's fine," Brighton said, without getting into too many details. Peg slowly pulled away from the curb and headed back to the school.

"Hey, Peg. So, you've been in this town quite a long time you said?" Kate asked.

"My whole life, born and raised," she responded proudly, strumming her hands on the steering wheel. "I know enough about this town to write a book." Kate looked back at Brighton with a smile.

"This sounds crazy, but by any chance, do you know anything about a witch that lived in town? I think it was quite a few years ago."

Brighton was perched on the edge of her seat, as far as her seat belt would allow her. When she heard Kate ask that question, she sunk back into the upholstered chair, stared out the window, and shook her head. This conversation was going to be interesting, she thought.

"A witch? As in practicing witchcraft? Oh heavens no."

"What about Lorna Karender? Does that ring a bell?" Kate asked.

Peg shook her head, laughing under her breath. "What do I look like? The town tour guide?" she said, her infectious laugh echoing in the car. "I bet you're talking about that book with poor Lorna's story. She was a strange gal, but she was no witch. She tried everything to support her family. I could remember my mom getting this salve from her; I still think it is the best thing to cure just about anything. She had a tough life. Lost a daughter—and her husband not too long after. Terrible shame. Just as terrible was how the people of the town turned on her so easily. They went from looking to Lorna when they needed a cure for some sickness, to shunning her and mocking the work that she did with natural medicine. That's how people are though. They can turn on you in a minute. I don't blame her for going into hiding. I think she had a son, too, but I never heard what happened to him. I believe he moved out of the area. Or he could be dead for all I know."

The school was in sight, and Brighton scrambled to get a few questions in before they left.

"Hey Peg, I know I read that Lorna's last name was Karender, but do you know what her maiden name was?"

Peg tapped her slender hands on the steering wheel. "I don't. She was with her husband for so long, we never heard about her life before that. I just know I still feel bad for that woman."

"Thanks, Peg. Maybe we will be requesting you again," Kate said as leaned back into the car.

"Anytime girls. It's been a pleasure. Uber driver and local historian at your service!"

Brighton knew that unless someone stumbled on the headstone in the cemetery, no one was aware of the other name attached to Lorna.

Kate and Brighton hurried to the entrance of the

school.

"I'll text my mom, and tell her we need a ride since we stayed late to work on our project," Kate said, without even lifting her head.

As they stood near the trophy case in the front of the school, Brighton didn't talk about their hospital visit. She was mentally drained after hearing Orwin was in the hospital and then talking to Peg about Lorna, it was all she could handle for the day.

"There she is. Ready?" Kate said, turning to Brighton. "Hey, obviously don't mention anything about Orwin, and let's not get into any conversations about the Lorna mystery, either."

"Oh, why, you think she might know something about the history in this town?" Brighton said, sounding surprised. She didn't think Kate and her family were here long enough to know much about the background.

"No, I don't want to get into it and hear a long, drawn-out lecture," she said, running to the car.

As Joelle drove them home, Brighton hoped her mom was home on time today. She didn't feel like being alone. As they pulled up, she didn't see a car in the driveway.

"Your mom isn't home yet? Do you want to come to our house instead?"

"No, I'll be fine. My mom will be back soon."

"Are you sure, Bright? You can eat dinner with

us."

"I'll call you later. Thanks." Brighton waved as she pushed the door open.

As the days grew shorter, she wished she or her mom remembered to leave a light on when they left the house. Brighton walked through the kitchen and living room, turning on every light possible. Luckily, the local news she tuned in to didn't have any reports of mysterious car crashes. Lighting from the refrigerator illuminated the kitchen even more, and she found a plate covered with foil. Attached to the top was a sticky note with a little heart scrawled in the center. While Brighton appreciated the gesture, it also meant she shouldn't expect her mom anytime soon. She wished her mom didn't have to stay late at work so often.

Brighton decided to heat her dinner after completing some homework. She settled on the couch reviewing notes for an upcoming test. That's when she noticed it. Buried under some old copies of tabloid magazines and newspapers, she saw the recognizable cover. *My Skull Possession* sat on the bottom of the pile. She thought she told her mom to get rid of it, but it probably got tossed aside. Brighton looked at the cover and studied the author's name. This time she felt like she had more of a connection as she noticed something else about the book. About halfway through, she saw a small card sticking out of the book. She slowly opened it and noticed a bookmark tucked in the crease. Brighton never continued reading long enough that she needed to save her place. Could her mother be reading it? Or did she happen to stick that randomly between the pages? Instinctively, she opened the book to the marked chapter.

As I sat at my dressing table, I stared at the reflection looking back at me. My nightly ritual of brushing my hair had also become one that could quickly turn into something of terror. As the sterling silver hair brush repeatedly smoothed my long golden strands, my hand froze in fear. I moved my face close to the mirror, trying to scrutinize the image before me intently. There was nothing there. I felt it. I felt the cold iciness surrounding the bones of my fingers, a subtle gripping force pressing against my wrist. But there was nothing there. Tears streamed down my face, as I slowly lowered my hand to the dressing table, the metal brush heavy in my grasp. Bottles of perfume rattled as I dropped the brush, and just as quickly, the presence disappeared. I did not bother to pick up my ornate monogrammed brush, for I feared it would bring back the invisible but foreboding entity. I vowed never to hold it again.

Brighton didn't like the visual she got after reading the passage. She slammed the book shut, maintaining the bookmark placement. Papers and magazines fluttered to the floor, as she tried to stash it beneath everything. Just as she finished arranging everything on the end table, it sounded like something fell. She looked at everything around her, and nothing seemed out of place. But she didn't mistake the crashing sound she heard. It sounded like it came from the kitchen. Brighton scanned the counter and table but didn't see anything out of the ordinary.

Her mother wouldn't be home for some time, so she figured she might as well heat her dinner now. As Brighton opened the stainless steel door, she was greeted by red, oozing gel dripping down the side of the door. She jumped out of the way as a broken jelly jar rolled onto the floor, completely shattering at her feet. That must have been the sound of the jar falling after shifting in the fridge. Brighton didn't think she moved too many things around when checking out her covered dish only minutes before. As she bent over to pick up the larger pieces of glass and wipe the rest with paper towels, she made the decision to call Kate.

"Hey, it's me. I think I might take you up on your offer if you don't mind. Would it be too much trouble to have your mom swing by and pick me up? It's dark out already."

She grabbed her bag and keys and waited outside on the porch for Laura to pick her up. She didn't feel like staying inside her house, and she had no intention of walking through the cemetery. The air was more than just crisp outside, and the biting cold seeped into the thin hooded sweatshirt. It was time to trade up for something a little warmer. Her heart skipped a beat as she heard a low cackling sound. She realized it was coming from next door, another addition to the ever-growing Halloween display. A lighted disc rotated, casting an eerie light on an animated witch, repeatedly stirring a large cauldron. As she listened to the shrill cackle, watching the hideous face turn from green to purple, she hurried down the steps as she saw Kate's mom pull up. She had never been so happy to see her.

Chapter Twenty-Three
Admitted

Kate sat on her bed, her legs drawn up close to her chest. She inspected her thumb, which she incessantly gnawed on for the entire time Brighton recounted her story.

"I'm sorry, Kate. I didn't want to upset you. But I don't have anyone else to share this with. I don't know what to think."

Kate stared at the bookshelf across the room. She untangled her legs and walked over to the shelf. Stretching on her toes, Kate reached past some of the items collected over the years. She pulled out a book and wiped away some invisible dust.

"All of my books like this are downstairs. You saw them on the shelves. My dad hated the idea of throwing any books away, but after my episode and stuff, they didn't want me exposed to any of it. Sure, I could get any of those books on my own or research unlimited online, but I promised them I wouldn't. I promised them I'd try to get better. But I couldn't get rid of all of them. I had to keep this," she said, sliding the book over to Brighton.

Brighton looked at the cover of the notebook. Inside it was filled with articles, postcards, and brochures.

They all had to do with the Myrtle Plantation. An image of two little girls in white dresses was glued to one of the pages.

"I saw them, Brighton, really I did. My parents thought I was crazy, but I promise you, I saw these little girls in the hallway. After doing research, I realized they were the little girls that died in that house," she said, rifling through pages. Kate tucked her hair behind her ears and frantically searched through the pages. "Look, here is another image of them." She turned the book toward Brighton, her eyes wide as she bit her bottom lip.

"Oh Kate, I didn't mean to do this to you. You don't need to revisit this," Brighton said as she leafed through the pages of articles and other papers Kate collected about the plantation. "You said it's a tourist attraction. Maybe they were kids visiting the plantation while you were there?"

"No!" Kate yelled. "Now you sound like everyone else. I know what I saw, and I know what I felt in that house. What I'm trying to tell you is that I understand. Does it mean the book is possessed? Did it cause jelly to fall out of your fridge and your lights to flicker? I don't know."

"Kate, I'm sorry. I know how you feel," Brighton said. She wanted to let her know she knew about her being institutionalized, but she didn't need to.

"No. You don't know, Brighton. You don't know

how they gave me so much medication that I couldn't see when they asked me to get up. You don't know how I sat in group sessions with people with serious problems, and I knew I was okay. You don't know how it felt to hear everyone whispering about my condition. I know what I saw. I know what happened. I'm not crazy, Brighton."

Brighton couldn't move and she didn't know what to say. Kate's hair was disheveled, her thin body folded into a tiny mound. Her confidence was gone, her vibrancy disappeared. Brighton walked over to Kate to let her know she believed her and that she did understand. She placed her own shaking hand onto Kate's heaving back.

Without any warning, Kate's door flew open. "Is everything okay? I thought I heard you yelling," Kate's mom said. As she looked back and forth at Kate and Brighton, she then turned her attention to the book sitting between them. "Kate, can I talk to you in the hall," she said, reaching down to pick up the journal brimming with articles and information.

Brighton couldn't make out the words they were saying, but she knew the conversation wasn't going well. As Kate came back into the room, she slowly closed the door behind her, leaning against it.

"My mom will take you home now if you don't mind. She doesn't want it to get too late. Do you think your mom is home?" she said, lifting her gaze to meet Brighton's. Her eyes were brimming with tears she was trying to hide. She secured her hair with an elastic band, trying her best to pull herself together. Brighton saved her any more embarrassment and grabbed her bag.

"I should go anyway. I have some homework to do." Kate gave her a weak smile as Brighton stopped before opening the door. "I'm sorry about this, Kate. I didn't mean for this to happen."

"It's fine," she whispered while leaning in to hug Brighton before she left. Her mom was waiting at the front door, keys in hand, looking very annoyed. "But I would still get rid of that book if I were you," she said. "I'll talk to you tomorrow."

Kate's body trembled as Brighton hugged her before leaving. She wanted to tell her how sorry she was about what she went through, especially resurrecting the fear that obviously still resided in her. Her forced smile couldn't hide what her eyes conveyed.

Brighton followed Kate's mom to the car and endured the short, quiet ride home. If she walked into her classroom in her pajamas, she couldn't feel more awkward then she did now. Her bag thudded on the ground, and she caught herself before tripping on the curb. After turning to wave to Kate's mom, she couldn't be happier to see lights on in the living room and her mom's car in the driveway.

Everything settled in around her like any other typical weeknight. She tossed her bag on the table. Her mom was sitting at the counter skimming through the newspaper and eating dinner.

"You didn't see your dinner in the refrigerator?" she asked, swinging her fork in front of her.

"I did, but I wasn't hungry then. I had to go over to Kate's anyway."

Brighton's mom stared at her plate as she moved the food around. The utensils clanked against the ceramic, amplified with the rest of the house in complete silence.

"Everything okay?" she asked, squinting at Brighton. "I'm sorry if I've been at the office a little more than usual in recent weeks. It is a busy time. I feel like something is bothering you."

Brighton contemplated explaining what she experienced when she was home alone. She knew her mother would give another rational explanation again, so she chose not to get into it. It was bad enough she had Kate worked up about the situation.

"No, everything is fine. Same thing here, just a lot of work to do for school." She turned to go upstairs to her room, but before she trudged up the stairs, stopped at the bottom step. "Oh, there is one thing. I was curious. Did you end up getting rid of *My Skull Possession*?"

Her mom paused a moment from eating forkfuls

of casserole and then held her fork up as if she had a revelation. "Mmmm, I meant to tell you that. I didn't get rid of it. I decided to read some of it to see what everyone is fussing about. It's around here somewhere," she said, looking around the kitchen. "I can find it if you need it."

"No, I was just wondering if you got rid of it altogether. What do you think of it?"

"It's okay. Different. I don't know about the rumors of it being the most horrifying book in recent times, but it's creepy. Not like anything else that's out there today, so maybe that's what makes it different and so popular. We both read some of it, and we're both still here."

Brighton rolled her eyes and turned to head upstairs.

"Oh, come here, Brighton. I'm kidding. Listen, if the book is making you that uncomfortable, I'll throw it out," her mom said, walking over to give a hug. "I still think you've been talking to Kate a little too much about this situation; but really, I'll get rid of it if it makes you feel better."

"I don't care if you read it. I'm better off if I read something a little more lighthearted."

"Well, it's almost Halloween. All of this hype will die down once this season passes. Everyone is obsessed with creepy decorations, visiting haunted houses, and hearing scary stories," she walked over to the window, parting the curtains with the side of her hand. "Did you see the neighbors keep adding to their display? I kind of like the witch."

Brighton didn't like the witch, and she doubted the passing of Halloween was going to make a difference regarding the odd events she kept experiencing.

"Yeah, the witch is neat. I'll be in my room," she said.

As Brighton entered her room, she immediately closed the window. It was getting colder every day; she wished her mom would quit opening it. As she fell onto her bed, she noticed she had several missed messages from Kate.

KD: Mom isn't happy that I kept that journal. She took it away from me.

KD: You there? Frustrated with all of this.

KD: Gets better. No more books. Call me when you can.

KD: Sorry about before. I'm okay. Didn't mean for you to see me like that. I'll be okay.

Brighton looked at the last text and wondered what she meant by that. No more books? Books about the supernatural? She assumed they didn't want her to relapse into her obsessive state again.

"Hey. What's going on?" Brighton asked as soon as Kate answered her phone.

"Well, so that's over. We don't have to worry

about any more deliveries at my dad's store."

Brighton felt like she was talking to a totally different person than just a few hours ago.

"What are you talking about?" Brighton asked.

"My dad is not carrying *My Skull Possession* anymore. I told you he said he was done. He said it's not worth the trouble."

"What trouble?"

"Not just with me, but that's part of it. My mom is aggravated I was starting to read into the paranormal genre a little too deeply again. But I guess my dad had a reporter stop by the store today. They wanted to do a story on the book, and how he was the only one selling it. They wanted his comments on the fact that some people died who read it. I guess they did some digging around. The reporter said when he started researching to find out the cause of death, that he noticed a trend. The causes of death in those cases came up inconclusive, and they were all from this town."

Brighton didn't answer immediately. She wondered why no one ever pointed that fact out before. Rumors swirled on social media, in the halls at school, and anytime a group of friends got together. But there was never anything official connecting the deaths besides the fact they read the book.

"My dad doesn't want to be associated with it any longer. At first, it was a novelty, but now it seems like he doesn't like the attention."

"Well, enough about the book. Are you sure you're okay? I was really worried about you. I hate seeing you upset."

"Really. I'm fine. All of that is in the past, it's my own stuff. Every now and then it gets the better of me, but I'm okay. Let's just forget about it."

The silence seemed to last forever.

"Brighton? Are you still there? Hello?"

"Oh well, like my mom was telling me before, maybe all of this hype will die down after Halloween. Speaking of, are you doing anything special tomorrow?" she asked, deciding to honor Kate's wishes, and forget about what happened back at her house.

"Not really. I thought you could come over here to pass out candy to trick-or-treaters. You said this street usually gets busy?"

"Yes. I'm not sure where half of the kids come from, but the street gets crowded. Most houses keep their lights on, too. It's fun."

"Sounds good. My mom will order pizza, and we can watch a few scary movies," Kate said.

Brighton usually liked Halloween, but this year she was ready to move on.

CHAPTER TWENTY-FOUR
HALLOWEEN

Brighton walked to Kate's house. Her mom offered to give her a ride, but on this night, she didn't mind making the trek in the dark. As expected, almost every house had a porch light on. Some homes were adorned with decorations while others had welcoming light guiding children to the front. Brighton smiled as she watched groups of young kids running from house to house. It brought back memories of when she was their age. Many of the families still lived on the same street, even though most had grown children. Kate's family was the newest family to move to this street. She forgot they had never experienced Halloween in their town.

As she neared Kate's house, she dodged the groups of kids running up the sidewalk. Lingering in front of the house were three boys who seemed a little too old to be trick-or-treating. They snickered as Brighton walked up the front porch steps. They were dressed in regular clothes but wore masks. They couldn't be much younger than Brighton, but she knew some kids like to push it each year to see if people were still willing to give them candy. As she was about to put her hand on the doorknob, she heard one of the boys laugh as he whispered to his friend. She froze and spun around to face them. They stood at the bottom of the porch, laughing and poking each other.

"I'm sorry, I didn't catch what you said," she said, as confidently as she could.

They continued to laugh until the boy repeated himself. "I hope I don't die from eating their candy. You know, the guy who lives there was the one selling those books. We wanted to see him firsthand," they said, laughing as they made their way down the street.

"Very funny," Brighton yelled after them.

Kate came out onto the porch with a bowl of candy. "What was that all about?" she asked, leaning over the porch, staring down the street.

"Oh, just a bunch of kids who are too old to be asking for candy. Told you it was busy," she said as another group of kids scampered up the steps. Brighton fished in the bowl for some chocolate bars and licorice, throwing them in the overflowing bags. "Happy Halloween," she said as she watched the little ninja, witch, and scarecrow jump down the stairs.

"You're right—it is busy on this street tonight. I like it though. It puts you in the spirit," she said as she reclined in the rocking chair.

Brighton figured they were going to stay outside to accommodate the constant stream of kids approaching the house. She thought it was probably best not to mention what the boys said, although they probably weren't the first ones to reference it. It wasn't hard to make the connection to the bookstore and the owner. It was a small town.

Before they headed back into the house, Kate put down the candy and gave Brighton a hug, whispering before she let go.

"Thanks for being my friend."

Brighton stood back, looked at her, and knew she didn't need to say anything else about her past. With that, Kate moved on as if nothing ever happened.

"So, don't mention anything to my parents about what I said yesterday," Kate said.

"You mean about not selling the books anymore?"

"Yeah, my dad was aggravated with the reporter. He didn't like how he attempted to connect him to what happened."

Brighton didn't respond. The rumors started circulating long before the reporter surfaced. She wondered why it didn't bother him after the second person died, and the connection was made he read the same book. But she figured she wouldn't mention anything and enjoy the night. As they passed out the last pack of Starbursts, they both headed back inside to watch Halloween movies on Netflix.

"It's getting late, but thanks again for having me over. It was fun." Brighton was happy to be able to disconnect from all of the worries that surrounded them in the past few days.

"Oh, yeah, by the way, I'm not sure if you saw, but Orwin's shop is open again. His nephew is running it for now. I guess Orwin is still in the hospital. I was thinking we should stop by so we could find out how he is doing. We can go right after school. I still don't want my mom knowing we are poking around that shop. We can do the same thing, and say we need a ride to that coffee shop, like you did last time, to work on a project. It's not too far from there. We can head over to Orwin's, and then get picked up at the coffee shop."

Kate seemed to have it all mapped out, so Brighton didn't have the heart to refuse.

Chapter Twenty-Five
They Have the Books

"What are you working on anyway? Don't you think it would be better to get together at the library or even at our house?" Laura Dorn questioned. Ever since she heard Kate's discussion the other night and about the reporter that was digging around, she seemed to monitor Kate's activities a little more closely.

"It's all good, Mom. I think when we all sit around with our coffee, just throwing ideas out there, we're more creative. When we get down to the mechanics of writing the paper, we'll be sure to be a little more studious," she said, glancing back at Brighton.

This explanation must have calmed her mom since she waved but waited to see them walk into the shop. Kate muttered something about going in for a second to make it look legitimate. Brighton followed her into the small store and watched as Laura seemed satisfied and drove away.

"Since we are here, we might as well get something. I've never been inside," Kate said as she took her coat off.

"Can I help you ladies with something?" the girl

behind the small counter asked. She didn't look much older than she and Kate, but Brighton didn't recognize her from school. Her brown hair had streaks of purple and was piled loosely on top of her head. She peered at Brighton over her large black-rimmed glasses, her amethyst nose piercing glinting in the fluorescent lights. Her dark-violet pout contrasted with her pale skin.

"This is our first time here, we're just looking around," Kate said as she walked up to the counter.

Brighton's gaze shifted to the chalkboard on the wall, studying the list of coffee flavors and specialty drinks. A small glass case contained a small selection of cookies and cake slices, but not a vast assortment. She listened as the girl droned on about how the beans are locally roasted, and the tea is blended nearby. They also had a few varieties of local honey.

The girl's customer service skills were about as welcoming as the surrounding atmosphere, but Brighton studied the board, deciding they should buy something since they were already here. As she reached into her pocket to grab some money, she froze. Sitting on the counter, neatly stacked next to small jars of honey and containers of pink and turquoise swirled candy sticks was a pile of books. As the girl droned on about the owner trying to keep everything local, Brighton's face felt hot, and the sound of her voice was drowned out by the blood pounding in her head. There weren't many copies, but there it was, the cold face staring back at her—*My Skull Possession*.

"Brighton? Earth to Brighton? Are you getting anything?" Kate asked. She looked puzzled as she stared at Brighton, but as Kate followed her gaze to the counter, she realized why Brighton looked troubled. They both stared at the books in front of them.

"Oh yeah, right? Wild that we have these," the cashier said, tapping her black-lacquered nails on the cover. "I don't know, I read it, and nothing happened to me. But all those other people? Weird. So, can I get you anything?"

Kate managed to say they would take a hot chocolate and cafe mocha. She scrawled their order on a small notepad, pushed the slip of paper through a square window and took Kate's money. Brighton watched as a hand grabbed the paper. As the person moved closer to the opening, she couldn't quite make out who it was, but his silhouette, completed with the swath of gray hair pulled back into a ponytail was unmistakable. Brighton trembled as they waited for their drinks. She watched as two thin bony hands slid their drinks forward through the opening. The lower part of his forearm had some wording tattooed in cursive. She couldn't make out what it said, and the person disappeared into the back room.

"Thanks," Kate said as she grabbed the drinks. The girl sat back down on a stool behind the counter, returning to her phone, her personality just as warm as when they walked in.

"Some study session, huh?" Kate said as she waited for traffic to clear as they tried to cross the street.

"We are still going to Orwin's?" Brighton asked as they briskly walked up the street. The Styrofoam cup warmed her hands.

"Yeah, but I'm going to text my mom and tell her she doesn't need to pick us up later. We can call Peg," she said.

As they continued their walk, Kate pondered how it was possible the coffee shop was selling copies of the book in their store. She tried to rationalize that due to the popularity of the book, it wasn't impossible customers bought books from her dad's store and then tried to resell them.

"Wait," she said, stopping in the middle of the sidewalk. "My dad processed all of his transactions through his register, but he also kept an old-school receipt book where he logged the customer's sale."

"Why would he do that?" Brighton asked.

"I don't know. That's how my dad always ran his business, and I guess when he finally took credit card sales and went electronic, he wanted to keep some of his old habits. But what I'm thinking, we can check back and see if someone came in multiple times and bought several copies of the book. I'm not sure what that is going to prove though. It's not like my dad had a contract with the author or a distributor, so he can't give someone a hard time about reselling the books. I mean, I guess if he wanted to give them a fight, he could..."

"Kate."

"... He could trace back who bought the books."

"Kate, listen to me. I think I know where they got their copies. I'm pretty sure the guy making our drinks back there was the guy I followed last week. The one on the bike."

"Come on, how can you be sure it was him? All we saw was a hand."

"I saw him, Kate. I'm sure that was him."

They continued to walk to Orwin's shop, neither saying much to each other. Some of the trees had a few leaves desperately hanging on to the branches. Brighton watched with each gust of wind as the remaining leaves slowly danced in the air and fluttered to the ground. Small piles of crimson, gold, and warm honey collected at their feet, giving more validation to fall marching toward winter. They only had a few blocks to go when Kate finally broke the silence.

"What do you think that means, Bright?" she asked.

"So, if he is the distributor of that book, I can understand why he tried to find another outlet. That coffee shop doesn't look like it gets much traffic. And you were there—I don't know how many repeat customers they get considering the environment. Maybe he saw the chance of hooking up with a nicer, more popular bookstore to get more sales. I can understand that. I wonder why he made such a big deal about keeping your dad as the *only* place to buy it. You would think he would try to get anyone on board that he could."

"I don't know. I don't think it's too weird. There aren't many non-chain bookshops in the area. Most specialty shops or chain bookstores want to know an authorized distributor backs the book. My dad probably saw it as something exclusive. He never expected what would follow, of course."

As they walked into the antique shop, nothing changed, but it seemed everything was missing. The dark walls and low lighting still felt subdued as they made their way through the store. The unusual collections of objects remained perched on glass shelves or were tucked away in corner cabinets. But what was missing was the cheerful and buoyant voice of Orwin.

"Hi. Let me know if I can help you with anything," the voice said from behind the counter. Orwin's nephew either realized that there were two girls in the shop, or he recognized them, as he jumped up from the book he was reading.

"Oh, hey. I know you. You came to visit my uncle."

"We were stopping in to see how Orwin was doing. Any improvement?" Kate asked.

Brett took off his cap and ran his fingers through his hair. "I told you how he was in and out of it for some time now, right? He would briefly wake. We would try to communicate with him, and he would only mumble. He keeps saying 'Coffee, coffee, coffee.' I never knew he drank that much caffeine. They tell him he can have all the coffee he wants if he wakes up."

"Wait, he's still not conscious? Is he going to be okay?" Brighton asked.

"He's been in and out of consciousness. Quite frankly, doctors still don't know what caused this episode. He hasn't been alert for days now. He's stable, just not communicating. They think it could be an issue with his nervous system, but they are running all sorts of tests. If you ask me, it just doesn't add up."

Brighton was sad to hear about Orwin. She was happy Brett was around to help keep the store going, as she worried what would happen to it while he was incapacitated. Brighton would hate to see it go under while he was getting better.

"Well, we will have to stop by the hospital soon to see him. I hope his condition improves. Oh, there's one more thing I wanted to ask. I'm not sure if you know this, but do you know where your uncle ended up getting those copies of *My Skull Possession*?" Kate asked.

Brighton could tell by the look on his face he was

annoyed.

"Look, I know what you're thinking. My uncle started selling those books, and then he got sick. You aren't the only ones asking about that. I had several people in here asking the same thing that knew the situation. And then they asked if we had the book in stock. I wasn't too close to my uncle, so I don't know the details about where he got the book, and quite frankly, I'm sick of hearing about it."

"Hey, we didn't mean to upset you. I'm sorry," Brighton said. She didn't try to explain why Kate questioned Orwin's source of obtaining the books. She figured it would cause more confusion and aggravation for his nephew. "Just let him know we are thinking about him if he wakes up. Here's my cell number. Can you call if anything changes?" she said, scribbling her number down on the back of one of the business cards. She held it out like a peace offering, hoping he wasn't too annoyed to refuse it. He grabbed it and stared at the card.

"Fine. I'll let you know when Orwin wakes up—if he wakes up," he said, thrusting the card into his jacket pocket. "Have a good day, ladies."

Kate pulled out her phone and started scrolling through her apps. "I guess we should see if Peg is available."

While Kate concentrated on setting up an Uber ride home, Brighton thought about their conversation with Brett.

"I'm thinking about what Brett said about *coffee* and *coffee shop* when Orwin was awake."

"Yeah, hopefully, he'll be okay, and we will be sure to get him as much good coffee as he wants. Preferable not from our little coffee shop down the road. Something a little better than that," Kate said.

"That's just it. I don't think Orwin was trying to say that he wanted a cup of coffee or he wanted to go to a coffee shop. I think he was trying to tell us something *about* a coffee shop."

CHAPTER TWENTY-SIX
NO FUNNY BUSINESS

It was a relief to see Peg pull up, waving to greet them. "My favorite fares. Glad to see you again, hop on in!" They both crawled into the small Honda and fastened their seat belts.

"Peg, is that Christmas music already?" Kate asked.

The sounds of Elvis singing "Blue Christmas" almost drowned out the sound of Kate speaking. As Peg reached over to turn down the volume, her bracelets clanked against the console. Instead of her other assortment of silver and beaded bangles, she wore four brightly colored holiday bracelets, adorned with presents, candy canes, and small rhinestone Christmas trees. She shook both of her hands in the air.

"That's right. As soon as Halloween is over, I start counting the days until Christmas. It's one of my favorite holidays," she said, pointing to her Christmas vest, complete with jewels and bows.

"Really? You could never tell," Kate said sarcastically.

"Oh, come on, it's never too early to get into the

spirit." They listened to a few more holiday favorites when they neared Kate's house.

About a block from her home, she placed her hand on Peg's shoulder.

"Stop. Right here is good," Kate said.

Brighton knew what she was doing. It was easier to saunter into the house unannounced, rather than have to explain why a strange car dropped her off. If her mom happened to be outside while Kate was walking down the street, it was a chance she would have to take.

Peg's car came to a sudden halt. She pulled over to the side of the road and pulled out her phone, mumbling to herself. "Kate, my dear. This isn't the address you put in, she said, glaring at the stretch of homes.

"I must have entered the wrong number. Sorry, Peg. Bright, are you coming over or headed straight home?"

"I think I'll go home. Talk to you later."

Kate slammed the door and slowly walked toward one of the homes. She fished in her pocket for her phone, acting as if she got a call. Brighton knew she was stalling.

"Should we wait for her to go in?" said their overprotective Uber driver. The small bells that adorned Peg's sweater rattled as she leaned over the seat to get a better view of Kate walking away from the car.

"No, she's fine. I'll text her later. You can just take

me home." Brighton said, trying to get her to keep moving. She knew Peg wasn't wholly sold on Kate's story. She slowly rolled forward, checking her mirror for signs of Kate entering her house. Brighton turned around to see her still playing into the charade.

"Well, if you say so. I like to make sure everyone gets home safe," Peg said, refocusing her sights on the road ahead. "And where is your house Miss, Bright, is it?"

"It's Brighton. My address is, um..." Brighton stalled, trying to think of a number to give a block away, but she wasn't sure if the house number would even exist.

Peg pulled over to the side of the road and parked the car. She turned down the music, so the sound of cheerful jingles and chiming was barely audible. She turned to look at Brighton, with a forced grin.

"Okay, Miss Brighton. I could believe that Kate punched in the wrong number, doubtful, but possible. But for you to forget your address when I asked? Something is going on. Listen, I think you're both nice girls, but I have to tell you, I have a pretty good rating as a driver, and I don't need to ruin that if you two have some funny business going on."

Brighton never thought Peg would suspect them of anything criminal or insidious. That was the furthest thing from her mind. But now she had to try to explain herself out of this one. She had no choice but to give Peg a little insight as to what was going on in her head.

"Peg, I can promise you, we aren't doing anything illegal or wrong. You have to trust me. But the thing we are working on isn't something our parents are a hundred percent on board with." She knew that didn't sound convincing, but Brighton didn't know precisely how to put it without giving too many details.

"I knew it. I'm sorry if it's something your parents aren't fond of. Chances are I don't want to be involved either. And frankly—" Peg preached before Brighton cut her off.

"Peg. I know you don't know Kate and me very well, but you have to trust me. I don't want to get into all of the details, but I will tell you this has to deal with *My Skull Possession*."

"That book everyone is going on and on about?"

"Yes. I'm just trying to find out a little more information about the author and maybe where the book came from. I asked you the other day if you had heard any stories about witchcraft in this town. You said you don't remember anything about Lorna before she was married?"

Peg looked down at the steering wheel, in deep thought. Brighton was happy she still wasn't stuck on the fact she and Kate were doing something that they shouldn't.

"I'm sorry. I don't remember much besides what

I told you the other day. She just had a tough go of it. And the people in the town weren't too nice to her. After her daughter Clara died and then her husband, it was all downhill from there."

"Wait, did you say Clara?" said Brighton.

"Yes. I think that was the little girl's name. Clara." As she spoke, recounting the same facts as the other day, Brighton only focused on one word—Clara.

"What do you think Lorna Karender had to do with that book?" Peg asked.

Brighton didn't want to get into the specifics, but she got more information than she expected from Peg. She couldn't wait to get home to call Kate. Luckily, as Peg rolled up near her house, Brighton felt as if she regained her trust. She gambled, hoping this time her mom wasn't home and gave Peg directions to her house. Brighton took her key from her bag and hurriedly opened the front door after they arrived. She waved back at a smiling Peg, who seemed reassured as she saw Brighton walk into the house.

Brighton ran up the stairs, scouring her room for the item she usually loathed seeing.

After her confirmation was correct, she grabbed her phone to call Kate. Just as she was about to hit send, she paused. Brighton wondered if this was the right thing to do. Was it fair to Kate to drag her into this, knowing the possibility of how she could become drawn into the situation? She didn't even have a chance to process what it meant to her or her town.

CHAPTER TWENTY-SEVEN
COMMON DENOMINATOR

The gym was quiet so early in the morning. Brighton decided to talk to Kate once they got to school. She decided against discussing her new information last night.

"But I thought you didn't believe in things like this?" Kate whispered.

"I don't—I usually don't. I guess I'm just not ruling anything out right now. If Lorna Karender is holding a curse over this town, we need to know why not everyone. Why a few select people?" From the look on her face, Brighton knew she got Kate's wheels turning. She just hoped it wasn't something she was going to regret. "So that's a huge part of it. And that is where I am going to need your help. Did you say your dad kept a paper record of his book sales too?"

"He did. I think I know where you're going with this. It will be too weird if I take those receipt books out of his store. He'll question what is going on. But, just this morning he was complaining about not feeling well. It may not work, but I can offer to close up the store for him. I can get back in my parents' good graces after all of this chaos the past few weeks. If I have just a little time, maybe I can comb through those books from the past few months."

"That's a lot to go through. I can get dropped off at the store if it works out. I'll help."

As a teacher looked in for the second time to see what was going on in the gym at this early hour, Brighton grabbed her bag and started heading for the door. "Let me know if it is a go or not, and I'll be sure to jot down all the info we have on the people we know of who died had a connection to the book."

Kate nodded, grabbed her bag and walked out.

As soon as Brighton returned home from school, she started making a list of names. It was a collaborative effort of data from her text messages and online obituaries. She realized how easy it could be for a story to get blown out of proportion.

While the news of an unexpected death generated interest and speculation, as soon as someone made a connection to *My Skull Possession,* stories spread like wildfire. The gossip, social media blasts and word of mouth conversations were enough to make it all believable. Brighton stopped to question her information. Information that didn't sit well with her for some time now. Kate was the one who contacted her every time there was news of someone else dying, and that they just read the book. But how did she know? Did her dad remember every face and name of each customer that purchased items from his store? And why did it all of a sudden begin when Kate and her family moved to town? If Kate never mentioned her stories of possessed items, if she never pointed out the odd connection to the untimely deaths and what they recently read, would the rumors have been so bad?

Brighton's hand shook as it hovered over the empty white page on the notebook. All of the messages she cross-referenced were from Kate. Brighton felt nauseous for what she was thinking, as well as disloyal. It was inconceivable, but possible that someone would do research on this little town and resurrect any connection to witchcraft. What if an unsuspecting self-published author was trying to do their promotion because they couldn't work with a traditional publisher? They were thrilled to have their work carried in a real bookstore, only to be taken advantage of and monopolized. Once the sales started to increase, they couldn't back away from continuing to supply the bookseller. Could Kate and her family hatch this entire plan? Maybe Orwin's suspicions and doubts were enough to land him in trouble. Kate was not very keen on returning to the hospital to visit him anytime soon. As Brighton sat on her bed, she was confused how she could go from feeling convinced there was a book in their town that had extreme supernatural influence, to the fact there was someone in town willing to manipulate stories and circumstances to their benefit.

Brighton traced the quilted pattern of the throw on the bottom of her bed, the swatches and shapes forming multi-colored diamond shapes. The material was soft and smooth and felt comforting as she ran her hand over the edges. She rested her head on her knees that were pulled close to her chest. She stared at the mirror in front of her. Just as she was studying the lines of the curved scroll-like edges of the mirror perched on top of her dresser, the strand of lights began to sway. It was slight, but it created a faint tapping sound as the lights hit the glass.

She decided not to overthink it this time as she bolted from her bed. She inspected the strand, to see if something had fallen causing the lights to move, but there was nothing out of place. As she stood in front of her mirror, she felt a cold draft against her back. She spun around to see it was not her mother that left the window open this time. The wooden window frame securely fit against the bottom sill. But that was when she noticed it. She reached up to feel the rough window frame hidden behind her lavender valance. The skin on the back of her hand encountered the same shock of cold air she felt across the room. She moved the valance to the side, causing her to sneeze from the dust gathered in the folds of material. Upon closer inspection, she realized that although the bottom window was securely flush with the windowsill, the top portion of the window had slid down about three inches. Since the valance obscured it, she wondered if this was the source of her feelings of coldness and undetermined noises. She tried pushing it up, only to have the old window slide back down. Maybe her mom noticed the same thing and also wanted to push it back to the correct position. As she stood back and stared at the window, she felt foolish knowing that old construction and a drafty pane could have explained a lot. She was shaken from her thoughts by a chiming sound. As she picked her phone up off of the bed, she saw her text messages.

KD: Okay for tonight. They agreed to let me close up the shop. Come over about 6:30 p.m.

Brighton stared at the phone, debating if she should respond—or show up for that matter. She picked up her phone and typed her response.

Brighton: I will see you after dinner. Thanks.

CHAPTER TWENTY-EIGHT
BACK TO THE CELLAR

"How late are you going to be?" Brighton's mom asked.

"I told her I would stay to help her close. You can pick me up around 9 p.m. She needed some help going through inventory forms for the end of the year," Brighton said. She struggled to only make small talk with her mom during dinner, her mind elsewhere. Brighton thought about all of the names mentioned in texts, Facebook conversations, and information from obituaries. There was also something else she noticed when doing her research. When the stories were recounted and retold, it was always pointed out that the individual seemed young to pass away so unexpectedly. But when Brighton milled through week after week of obituaries, others from the surrounding area appeared to have died prematurely. She wondered why they weren't grouped in with this supernatural madness. As for tonight, the plan was to scour the paper records from the past few months, looking for a match of book sales confirmed with names scrawled into her book.

"Well, if you're ready, I can drop you off now," Laura said

Brighton ran upstairs to grab her phone, bag, and notebooks. She was sure she was going to get some answers tonight.

As Brighton approached The Book Cellar, she noticed tiny white lights framing the large picture windows. Several stands were situated near the glass, supporting cookbooks, best sellers, and colorful children's selections. It looked like preparation for the upcoming holiday season started early.

"Hey, glad you were able to come over. I started setting up the front window in preparation for the holidays. You can never start too early. I saw Christmas decorations out in some of the stores before Halloween."

Brighton followed her to the back of the store and pulled up a stool next to the counter. Overflowing on the glass countertop were boxes of small receipt books, their charcoal carbon slips sticking haphazardly out of the edges.

"That's a lot to go through," Brighton said, thumbing through the many names, her fingers looked like she handled a chunk of coal.

"Those are done," Kate said.

"Oh, you already have a list of names?" Brighton asked. She thought Kate wanted her to research the list.

"It wasn't that hard to find. Between all of the texts back and forth, the countless forums and conspiracies that circulated, it was pretty easy to track down all of the names."

Brighton thought she would just put it out there right from the start. "Speaking of which, how were you able to find out those particular people who died read *My Skull Possession* or had the book?"

Kate pulled another box from beneath the counter, looking at the small tablet in front of her as she flipped through the pages.

"What do you mean? It's all everyone was talking about. Don't forget Sherry's dad, too. I didn't talk to her directly, but the cousin said that not long before he died, he just finished reading the book. He was in the hospital for a few days. They didn't find him like the others."

"I forgot that was Sherry's dad. Once she came back to school, no one wanted to say anything about it to her. It was too weird."

As she talked out loud, she realized it wasn't too outlandish Kate would know all of the details. Sherry's relative was the one who gave them the news, and as Brighton scanned through her notes, she realized Kate's dad knew one of the medics who worked nightshift for the volunteer ambulance crew. He just happened to be on the scene of the fatal one car accident. Brighton's head was spinning; overwhelmed with an onslaught of information that was leading her in too many directions.

She watched as Kate meticulously ran her finger over each slip of paper like she was working on an assembly line. Her hair wasn't pulled back and hung over her shoulders every time she leaned forward to inspect another receipt. Brighton felt ashamed about how quickly doubt could surface and overtake her mind, without all of the facts. Kate may have had a quirky past, but she had been a real friend since she moved here. She wasn't sure what to believe, but she did feel in her heart that Kate considered her a true friend.

"Here, let me take some of those," Brighton said, leaning over to grab a few of the shoeboxes. They were only interrupted by a few customers, some browsing, others looking for specific books. As it neared 8:30 p.m., they pulled out the last two boxes. As of now, neither Kate nor Brighton found any match of the names. It was possible a slip wasn't filled out, but it was usually just Kate's parents or Kate who tended to the customers. She said her dad was pretty adamant about keeping the paper records. From the volume of names in chronological order, Brighton believed this to be true. They each grabbed a record book, and then gently placed them back in the box. Either all of the names they were looking for just happened to be missed during their transaction or the books weren't purchased from The Book Cellar. Brighton wasn't sure which answer was more disturbing.

"My mom will be here soon," Brighton said, as Kate furiously checked the books one more time.

"I don't understand. My dad was very diligent

about keeping a paper record. It's something he continued with even after he got his computer system. I can't imagine he would miss these. The only name I found is the guy from the accident."

Brighton's thoughts wavered back and forth. She was so unsure about what to believe. She realized it was best not to pass judgment on anything at this moment. Right now, their focus was on finding the records, and they weren't having much success in doing so. Although they could have been omitted on purpose, Brighton didn't want to go down that road. As she watched her friend unsuccessfully search through name after name, she figured Kate sensed Brighton's doubt and was trying to prove her wrong.

"Kate, it's okay. Please stop."

Kate pushed the boxes aside and covered her face with her hands. Brighton could tell she was crying.

"Hey, Kate, really, it's okay," Brighton said, hugging her friend.

"I know. I just thought if we could find something, it would lead us to more answers. I didn't want you to think they were omitted on purpose," Kate said, reading Brighton's mind. "Quite frankly, I wish my dad never sold the stupid book. It's just causing too much trouble."

As Brighton tried to console Kate, she realized there was only one place they needed to check next. Her gut told her the names weren't missing. If it was true people that met an untimely death did have a copy of *My Skull Possession*, they didn't get it from The Book Cellar.

"But if the book has some supernatural attachment, why does it matter where they came from?" Kate asked.

"There are only two places people could have gotten it. We need to go back to the coffee shop and also pay a visit to Orwin," Brighton said. "Tomorrow morning, I think you need to stop by the hospital to see Orwin, and I'll swing by the coffee shop."

CHAPTER TWENTY-NINE
RICHARD

The next day, Kate and Brighton decided to split up. At the coffee shop, Brighton waited at the counter to see the girl with the purple hair appear. She was surprised when someone else came to the register. It was the man who worked in the back preparing drinks the other day.

"Can I help you with something?" he said.

It was the first time that Brighton saw his face. His eyes were the palest ice blue, with a hint of smoky gray. The deep furrows in his brow and lines in his face made him look tired. A few stray strands of stubborn gray hair fell away from the slick ponytail that was pulled back tight. While the girl with the purple hair wasn't the most engaging and pleasant the other day, she at least looked presentable, albeit in a quirky kind of way. Instead, she was greeted by someone who looked like he just rolled out of bed. His faded gray long-sleeved shirt was wrinkled, and his jeans were threadbare and worn. When he turned to grab something from underneath the counter, she studied his profile. It was the same person who delivered books to The Book Cellar and the same person she followed back to his home. She needed to think quickly. Brighton could tell he was getting impatient with her as she stared at the chalkboard.

"Umm, I think I'll have a toasted almond coffee," she said.

The man behind the counter took a Styrofoam cup and pulled the lever to fill it with the aromatic steaming liquid from its container. As he looked for the correct lid, Brighton figured it couldn't hurt to ask.

"So, these books here. How did you possibly get your hands on them?" she said, hoping she quelled the nervousness in her voice as best as possible. She looked at the long gray ponytail and waited for him to turn around. He paused, standing still and holding the lid to the cup. After a few moments, he secured the top and placed it in front of Brighton. He smiled when he looked up at her, revealing teeth that seemed to be yellowed from excessive coffee drinking or too much smoking. The smell of stale cigarettes appeared to indicate the latter.

"Yeah, well, someone came in asking if I would carry them here. "I didn't know nothing about them, but I told him it would be all right. Is that all I can get for ya?"

"Who was it exactly? I've been trying to find some information about the author, and now it sounds like you can't even buy the book anywhere else. You know there are stories about bad things that happen to some people who read it," she said, pushing her luck. Her voice cracked, and she cleared her throat, trying to disguise her nervousness.

"Listen, the books are there if you want to buy one. I can't help you with anything else about it. I'm sorry."

He averted eye contact with Brighton and crossed his arms waiting for a response. He pushed his sleeve up as he scratched his forearm, revealing the tattoo Brighton caught a glimpse of when he was passing their drinks through the serving window. But this time she was able to make out what the inscription said. Her eyes lingered on the word, and he pulled his sleeve down, holding his hands behind his back.

"Umm, I'm good, just the coffee is fine, thanks," she said.

The man stared at her as he took her money. This time his gaze did not shift from her eyes. His cold stare made her uncomfortable, so she grabbed her coffee and headed to the door.

As she exited the store, juggling her coffee to grab her phone to call Kate, she recalled how over the past few days there weren't many things she felt confident about. But there was one thing of which she was very clear. The man at the coffee shop most undoubtedly knew more about the book than he said. Brighton was determined to find out what he was keeping from her.

Every time she attempted to make a call, it would

end. She immediately reached Kate's voicemail on the next try but didn't want to leave a message. She needed to talk to Kate. Just as she was about to give up, her phone rang.

"Bright, I've been trying to call you! What is wrong with your phone?"

"I was just going to say the same thing. Listen. I have something to tell you, but I'll explain everything later. I need to do a little more digging," Brighton said.

"What? I can barely hear you. I have great news. It's Orwin. He's awake! They are still running tests to see what caused him to be so sick, but at least he is conscious. But Bright, you were right. He wasn't asking us for coffee. He was saying the coffee shop. That is where he bought his books. It wasn't from my dad's store. Orwin didn't get a good feeling about Richard."

"Who's Richard?" Brighton asked. She could barely hear Kate's muffled tone.

"The owner of the coffee shop. Orwin happened to stop in one day and noticed the books for sale on the counter. You know Orwin; he didn't want to let an opportunity pass him by. He wanted to buy more, but Richard said he needed to save some for his customers."

"Well, I think he has a deeper connection to My Skull Possession than we think, even though he admits to knowing nothing about the book. And I am 99 percent sure he was your delivery guy. I'm going to try to find that out for sure. Kate? Kate?"

Brighton's connection cut out, and the call dropped. She rarely had trouble with her phone. What timing. She knew she could fill her in when they met up later. Brighton couldn't wait to recap her visit to the coffee shop and tell Kate about the other stop she was about to make.

Chapter Thirty
Buzz Buzz

"Thanks, Peg. I promise I'll get the app downloaded on my phone. I'm glad I kept your number, though. I hope this is enough," she said as she handed Peg the crumpled dollars.

"No worries, I enjoy seeing you and Kate. Where is she? Is she working at the register?" Peg said, holding her hand up to shield the sun while staring at the store.

"Oh, no, she should be here soon. Thanks again, Peg!" Brighton waited until she drove off and then she hurried around to the back of the store.

The bike was still in the same place, and she pedaled as fast as she could. The sun was warm on her face, but it wasn't enough to thaw her frozen skin. She knew Richard wouldn't be home since he was at the coffee shop, but she only wanted to look around his property. If he had as many cases of books to supply The Book Cellar and his store, there had to be some evidence of boxes or packing materials. No one ever said she couldn't take a peek in the windows and take a look around. Sure, it might be considered trespassing, but Brighton didn't think many people would be around to worry about it.

The houses she passed had lights on and cars in

the driveway. Knowing neighbors were at home made Brighton feel better about her second trip to the isolated house. As she approached the long drive, she debated if she should stash the bike again or ride up to the porch. Although Brighton knew no one was home, she tried to be as inconspicuous as possible. She leaned her bike against the trunk of a pine tree, the low branches draping over the handlebars. She jogged up the rest of the drive and turned to be sure no one else was coming. Richard, as she now knew him, would be on a bicycle, so it wouldn't be as easy to hear him coming.

More leaves had fallen since the last time she was here. The trees were becoming barren, showing that fall was slowly slipping away to make way for what was forecast to be a cold winter. Brighton's fingers were numb; this cold Saturday felt like winter had already set in. She approached the house and didn't see anything out of the ordinary. She made her way over to the back of the house and stopped as she noticed how quiet it was. She looked at the lines of shrubs and found it unusual he would maintain landscaping in the middle of the woods. As she moved closer, she approached the strange, cube-shaped pieces arranged in a straight line. They were wrapped in black insulation, and Brighton didn't want to disturb it since they seemed to be tightly secured.

There were no signs of shipping boxes or packing material strewn about the yard. An inspection of the two green garbage cans turned up empty as well. She wasn't sure what she expected as if he would have boxes piled up with a large sticker indicating its contents. She tried peering in the windows, but the curtains were drawn. A wind chime was protected from any buffeting winds and startled Brighton as she accidentally hit it with her head. The chiming clamor broke the silence around her, and also caused her to jump back, slamming against the door. She heard the hinges squeak and watched as the door slowly opened. The sound of the chimes didn't seem as loud as the thumping of her heart. There were no lights on, and she was reasonably sure Richard lived alone.

"Hello?" she said, poking her head into the door frame. She hoped no one would answer but felt better if she checked. Turning on her phone flashlight, she looked around and found the home to be sparsely decorated, but very tidy. Sure enough, she saw boxes lining the wall of the kitchen. She reached in to pull out the book that has caused her so much turmoil over the past few months. But not as much as it did for others. She could confirm Richard was the one distributing the books, but wondered why he didn't want to admit to it? Could it be that like Kate's dad, he tried to distance himself from all the negativity that surrounded *My Skull Possession*? Brighton looked at the papers and mail neatly stacked on the counter. The name Richard Karen was on all of the mailers.

As she sorted through them, she saw a bookcase underneath the kitchen counter. There were rows and rows of books about the supernatural, possessions, and unexplained haunted occurrences. On top of the three-tiered shelf were small picture frames. The first picture was of an old woman sitting in a rocking chair. She didn't face the camera, but instead, the image captured a profile of a woman with her hair pulled back tightly into a bun, her gnarled wrinkled fingers grasping a shawl around her shoulders. The photo was black and white but photographed recently. The other two photos were also black and white but faded and much older. The two children sat on their parents' laps—they couldn't be more than two years old. The last picture Brighton picked up was of a young girl. There was no mistaking who she was. Underneath the faded photograph of the thin, blond girl was a name written with blue marker, Clara. The same name forever etched on Richard's arm.

Brighton held the small frame as she inspected the kitchen. In every cabinet, she found small clear bottles, lids, and containers with white labels affixed to them. She reached up to grab one of the cylinder containers to inspect the words scrawled on it. Black. She grabbed another. Green. She wondered if it contained paint, but by the heft of it, it felt a lot lighter. She shook the contents and unscrewed the lid. Inside, Brighton found tea leaves. Behind the large canisters were smaller ones, stout and round. The labeled assortment ranged from everything from Echinacea to lemongrass. Spices and tiny glass bottles of flavorings rounded out space in the rest of the cabinet. It looked like someone made unique tea blends.

She crouched down to find the lower shelves stocked with unlabeled jars of honey. In the recesses of the cabinet was a crumpled brown bag. Brighton reached back to grab it and pulled it into the light. There were several jars labeled "Rhododendron," "Azalea," and "special honey." Just as she was reaching back for the second bag, she thought she heard the sound of a car pulling up. Brighton's stomach dropped after a glance out the window verified what she feared—someone was pulling up the drive. She assumed Richard lived alone and that he didn't drive. Unfortunately, she was wrong on both accounts. It was too late to dash out the door. She would surely be spotted. There was a chance she could make it to one of the neighbor's houses, but she wouldn't get far on her bike. She slid between the cabinet and some boxes, stacking a few others in front of her.

There was no heat on in the small home, but a river of sweat ran down Brighton's back. The arches of her feet burned as she pulled her knees as close as possible to her chest, teetering on the balls of her feet. She listened to the unmistakable roar of an engine, but no one silenced it. There was no slamming of a door, the car just sat and idled. Maybe he came back because he forgot something and, hopefully, it was outside the house. She waited for what seemed like hours, but probably amounted to only a few minutes. Then the car drove away. When Brighton was confident it was gone, she waited another ten minutes to be sure the vehicle left. She looked out the window to check for the car. There was no one outside, but she knew it was time to go. Brighton replaced the bag into the cabinet, and carefully placed the pictures on top of the shelf. Just as she turned out the light, she saw a shadow pass by the window. There was no time to return to her hiding place, so Brighton ducked down behind the counter. While she would probably be discovered, she could try to make a run for it when she had the chance. This time, she didn't have to wait as long.

Chapter Thirty-One
Momma

"Hellooooo," a male voice called out. The hinges squeaked as the door shut. She heard the deliberate thud of footsteps, the clang of drawers and cabinets slamming shut, and another door slowly brushed across the threshold. Maybe he was going to the bathroom, and this could be her chance to make a run for it. She leaned forward, only to be greeted by a pair of beat-up old sneakers.

"Hi. I figured I'd be seeing you again, but not in my house. I guess that wasn't you backing out of my driveway." The broken hinge sounded like old bedspring as he grasped it and shook the frame. "Front door was wide open. I knew something was up."

Brighton slowly inched up the wall behind her to a standing position. She knew she had no explanation for being here.

Richard placed a hand on one of her shoulders. The smell of cigarettes and something earthy filled her nostrils.

"Relax, dear, you're going to take a seat at the table. Now after our conversation at the coffee shop, I figured you would be digging around. You took me by surprise snooping around this place though. Find what you want?"

Brighton's voice trembled as she looked at the table. "I just wanted to know why you didn't tell me you were selling those books. I only wanted to see if you were storing them here. Please, I just want to go home. I promise I won't bother you about the books anymore."

"Oh no, no, no. I know you won't let it go that easily. I saw you staring at this today," Richard said, pointing at his arm. He traced his thin finger over the name, his stained fingernail stopping at the first letter. "I'm sure you made that connection hours ago, right?"

The name Clara was tattooed on him, as well as the dedication written at the beginning of the book. She knew it associated him with the book, but she didn't realize the direct connection.

"Look, I'm just going to get going," she said, slowly getting out of her chair.

"I told you to sit down," Richard said, slamming his fist on the table. "And put your phone in front of you."

She slid her phone out of her pocket and placed it at the center of the worn wooden table.

"Let me give you a little background on ol' Richard Karen. My father died when I was eleven, my sister died when I was eleven, and my momma lived until she was almost ninety."

"Sorry about your dad and sister," Brighton mumbled.

"Sorry? Well, thank you kindly. It's too bad everyone wasn't sorry. We wouldn't be where we are today, now would we?"

"I don't know what you mean."

"Well, I'll tell you what it means. The first decade of my life was just fine. My momma was one of the most popular ladies in town. She was able to mix up the best healing herbs and medicines to treat all kinds of sickness. She was no doctor, but she knew the natural benefits of everything. They always joked Lorna could get you the best potion for whatever was bothering ya. She made a decent living doing this, and our family was happy."

"Sounds like you had a real nice family."

Richard did not accept her olive branch, rolled his eyes, and continued with his story.

"When Momma wasn't helping others, she would write her books. She always said she had a story to tell, and would one day sell her books, too. That was her dream. So jump ahead a few years and the Karender family good fortune took a bad turn. My little sister, Clara, got real sick. Momma tried everything to help her, but it wasn't working. She planned on getting her to the doctors, but it was too late. Later that year, my daddy passed away at only forty-one. I think it was from a broken heart."

Richard's eyes glazed over, and he slowly nodded his head while recounting his sad childhood.

Brighton knew this story already, and she knew where he was going with this. It was almost like he was explaining the events from the book she read at Kate's store. As Richard told the rest of the story, he detailed the same tale of how everyone in town turned on Lorna and accused her of killing her husband and daughter.

"All those years my momma helped everyone in town, and then you only need one person to start gossipin', and all of a sudden she's practicing witchcraft. When she needed people to help her the most, they abandoned her."

As Richard told the story, she could hear the pain in his voice. Reading the story at the bookstore made it sound like another urban legend in town. Hearing Richard give examples of neighbors and friends turning their heads and hearts made Brighton feel sorry for not only Lorna but for Richard, too.   It finally clicked with her it could be Lorna or Clara supernaturally attached to these books.

"Is that why you are selling these books? Helping to fulfill your mother's dream of selling her book, and bringing your mom and sister back?" she asked.

Richard put his head down on the table. She heard a low guttural laugh that grew louder and louder. "Yes, yes, that sounds perfect. Doesn't that sound text book perfect? A man gets his revenge by selling his poor mother's book, who suffered her whole life, and then somehow conjuring her back from the dead, allowing a portal for the spirits also to get their revenge!" he said continuing to laugh.

Brighton shrugged her shoulders, knowing it sounded ludicrous, but didn't think anything was too crazy after the past few weeks.

"Well, that's what I wanted everyone to think," he said, slamming both hands on the table. "And part of that is true. I wanted to get my momma's book out there once and for all, and I wanted to get revenge for all those people being so mean to her. She lost my dad, and she lost my sister, and I had to spend my life growing up watching her go crazy. All the loss and disappointment took a toll on her, and she never recovered."

Richard stared at the table. His weary face reflected more sadness than anger. Brighton realized how hurt he was, and thought maybe she could have him vent some of his frustration into telling his story. She could get him to talk to her rationally.

"You said part of that was true," Brighton said, lowering her voice.

"Yes, indeed. I know there are books out there that talked about my momma and this town, the very one I'm sure you read. She never practiced no witchcraft, I'll tell you that. But she did know her herbs," he said with a smile. "One of the only things she had left in her life was her writin'. She had a heck of a story to tell and I figured that was the least I could do for her. When I decided to get the book printed, I had as hard of a time getting it out there for sale, rejected, just like she had been all her life. The printer had me upside down on all the money I shelled out to print the books, and I was just about to give up when a new family moved into town and opened an independent bookstore. I tried my luck, and when Mr. Dorn agreed to be the one to carry my books exclusively, I was thrilled."

Brighton watched as Richard sat across from her, his arm resting on the table, his leg extended beyond the chair. As he talked about his mother, his gaze focused on the bookshelf across from them, but Brighton knew that wasn't his fixation. Lost somewhere in Richard's head was a small boy who had a tough life. Knowing this didn't make Brighton feel any safer. She glanced over at the door and knew she needed to get out. She didn't notice a weapon, but couldn't tell what he had stashed in the trailer or even in his pockets. As he paused, slightly nodding his head, all she could hear was the ticking of a clock. The light metal of the wind chime tinkled peacefully with every gust of wind outside—how Brighton wished she was out there.

"So, you believe in all this supernatural stuff?" he said, jolting himself back into the present and folding his hands on the table. "You believe things move by themselves, spirits attach themselves to objects, and come back to give us folks here a hard time?" he said grinning, as he waited for a response.

"I...I don't know what I believe. I guess it can happen."

Richard stood up and held his finger up as if she should wait. She contemplated pushing him out of the way but didn't know if that would put her in greater danger. He rummaged in the cabinet taking out the brown bag Brighton saw before. There was another stack of boxes in the corner behind a couch, and Richard grabbed the top one and placed everything on the table in front of her. He sat down, methodically taking out bottles and bags, lining them up on the table.

"I got my momma's book out there for her, but I helped her with something else," he said. "Sweet revenge."

Brighton stared at the collection in front of her. Her mind clouded with stories of witchcraft and spells.

"Could this be possible?" she thought.

Her chest heaved as she studied the array of bottles, herbs, and small bags in front of her. What if this was the answer all along? Did this rank up there with all the stories of dolls and vases? Maybe Richard not only fulfilled his mom's dream of selling her book, but he also found a way to channel her witchcraft and somehow make My Skull Possession an object with the power to possess. It could bring back Lorna Rellim Karender, allowing her to seek her revenge on the very town that shunned her years ago. Richard's voice sounded distant, and Brighton tried to stop the room from tilting.

"Do you believe in the ability for something evil to transfer its energy into something as simple as a book?" she pried.

Richard continued taking jars and packets out of the bag. "When I talked to Mr. Dorn, I made it so he agreed to be the only one selling my books. Of course, I sold some in my store, too. But he had more of a reach than I did. Once word got out of what was happening to some of these poor souls who read My Skull Possession, it was sure to create a buzz, so to speak. And when the buzz got too negative, or people like you and your friend Kate started nosing around, I would have nothing to do with it. They would look at where the books came from. The place everyone was talking about. Sole distributor. No one talkin' about a little ole' coffee shop sellin' a couple of things on the counter."

"People usually don't blame bad luck on books."

"No, but if the truth ever came out, it would have been the new business owner who just moved to town. No one knew much about him or his family, and if they did some diggin', they'd find the reason they moved was their crazy daughter was talkin' to spirits before coming to Bradertown. Oh yeah, I did my research all right. Now by the time someone found out my story, I would be long gone."

"What story?" she asked, her voice trembling.

"Growing up with momma, she let me help her make all kinds of medicines using different herbs and spices, just like the ones you see here," he said, pointing to the jars on the table. "I knew what was good—and what was not so good." He stood up and walked over to the door, crossing his arms and staring back at Brighton.

"Notice all my lovely hedges outside? Looks mighty nice when they are in bloom. The bees especially like it. I make sure that's the only place they can go to pollinate. Momma always loved the bright colors of the rhododendron and azalea bushes. Thankfully, the bees liked them as much, too."

He sat back down and picked up some of the packets. "So, in my little shop, you noticed there were a few things that I sold: coffee, tea, and books, of course. Momma's book."

Brighton wasn't sure where he was going with this. She wondered if he was able to use these concoctions to put a spell on the books.

"Not sure if you know the story, but centuries ago, there was a king who knew how to take down a whole army without a sword."

Brighton thought Richard was surely losing his mind. She stared at the door, looking to escape.

"Please stop staring at that door, Miss. You're gonna want to hear the rest of this story since you're so curious and love sticking your nose where it doesn't belong. I have to admit, I'm mighty proud of how this all went down. Momma would be so proud of me. You are talking to a real mastermind here. So, as it goes, there is a certain type of rhododendron that contains what is called a Grayanotoxin. It's rare, but they grow in the countryside of Turkey. Bees that pollinated from those flowers produced honey highly concentrated with this toxin. The king gave the honey to the soldiers. It killed some of them and made the rest of the men easy prey."

"What does this have to do with a haunted book? Were people hallucinating when they read it? I don't understand," Brighton whispered.

Richard picked up one of the packets, shaking the contents. "The coffee, tea, and honey in my store are made by none other than yours truly. Picture this if you will," he said, jumping up, spreading his hands out, eyes wide.

"Good ole' Mr. Dorn starts selling My Skull Possession. My first job is working day and night, going into as many online forums and book review sites as I possibly could, starting to plant the seed. Making people think there was a story behind it and that it was said to have supernatural attachment and special powers. And then, whattaya know? You create a buzz and demand. It got people's interest. I built it up, creating a frenzy of people talking about where you can get this book, and what happened when you read it. Of course, nothing happened after they read it."

"Nothing happens?"

"Nothing until Thomas Regal. Earl Grey drinker I believe. Comes in one day, like many others before him, and orders tea. As he is standing at the counter, he notices the copy of My Skull Possession on the counter. 'Hey, that's the book everyone is talking about, right?' and BINGO," Richard screamed. He walked over to the table, and crouched down low, next to Brighton's chair. "We got ourselves the perfect candidate. Now would it work? I don't know, but I had to start tryin'."

His face was close to Brighton, the smell of cigarettes was so strong it was as if smoke was blown in her face. He paced back and forth, reaching on top of the refrigerator.

"Mind if I smoke?" he said out of the corner of his mouth, flicking the plastic purple lighter. Brighton sat silently.

"So, I got myself a tea drinker, interested in the book, and I made my push. I talked up that book like it was the best thing since sliced bread, how hard it was to get, we only had so many copies. Can't refuse that now. And then I mentioned how we also had some locally blended tea and coffee, and 'Oh, I see you are a tea drinker, you need to try this. It boosts your immunity and when you match that up with this honey, and you got yourself a real winner,'" Richard said, dragging a chair across the floor, taking a seat.

Richard grabbed an old coffee cup from the counter behind him and tapped the ashes from his cigarette. He tipped back on his chair, and reached behind, his hand fishing for something on the bookshelf. His gaze never left Brighton as he exhaled a stream of smoke.

"Here," he said while flipping through pages, his cigarette hanging out of his mouth. "Mr. Regal not only went home with this, but he also loved the idea of the tea AND the honey," he said, tapping his finger on the book and placing it back on the table. "I'll tell you. I didn't know what to expect. I read about the ones you stay away from, and how they could make you sick, but it would take a huge concentration to make someone sick. I mean they would have to drink that tea and honey every day. And let me tell ya, the first time, the very first time, it would only be a small dose. They would get a little buzz from it. So they would feel good and try it again. By then, it would start working on the nervous system, bring the blood pressure down, and affect the heart. By the time someone landed in the hospital, they'd think it was a heart issue or a stroke."

Brighton's voice was barely above a whisper. "How many people did you sell it to? Wouldn't we have heard about a lot of people getting sick or dying?"

"That's just it. I didn't know what to expect. As I said, it depended on the person's health before that, how much they drank of it. For all I know, they could have tried it once and then threw it out. I had to get it out there as much as possible. And after poor Mr. Regal, bless his heart, well, I just went with it from there."

Brighton stared at Richard across the table. She couldn't believe what she was hearing, but she had a hard time processing precisely what he had done. All she knew was she needed to get out of this house. While he seemed pleased to boast about his acts, she doubted he would let her walk away with that information.

"Didn't you ever worry about someone tracing it back to you?"

He crushed out the cigarette, and got up, blocking the door. He leaned against the frame, staring at the ceiling.

"When I tell you I spent all my hours reaching out to forums, creating usernames, responding to other people, it's all I did. And then once I drilled it into everyone that, hey, this guy read My Skull Possession and the curse must be true since he died after reading it, the thing spread like wildfire. People love conspiracies. They love anything having to do with the supernatural. Pair that with making this book so hard to get, and you got yourself a demand. The idea that the book could be cursed or haunted and be the cause of all these people dying made people curious. And where did they flock? Who got all the publicity?"

"Mr. Dorn's shop," Brighton said. She realized what he did. Most people thought you could only get the book at The Book Cellar. If they happened upon it else-where, most people still assumed you could get it at Mr. Dorn's. And there was nothing fishy going on there. They bought the book, and that was that.

"That's right. And no one would ever make a con-nection they were poisoned. The only common denomi-nator was they had that book. And everyone all over the internet said it had to be something supernatural. And if it got to the point they needed someone to blame, well, a new store owner with an unknown history and a crazy daughter moves into town, they must be the reason all of this happened. Believe me. I was ready to cover my tracks from all angles."

"But you sold books to the owner of the curiosity shop? And he's still alive. He was selling your books."

Richard looked out one of the small windows. "Yeah, Orwin made things a little difficult. It's okay, though, from what I've heard, he is still in the hospital and not doin' too good. I think he was affected by the tea I sold him, so the chances are that fat little man is not waking up anytime soon."

She realized Richard didn't know Orwin was

awake.

"He almost screwed me up real good. I wasn't in the shop the day he bought all those books. The girl I have working there didn't know what was going on, so when he came in and bought a bunch of copies, I wasn't there to upsell my special tea and honey. He came back a few days later looking for more. I told him we were out, and that's when we started talking about the coffee and tea I had for sale. He was a hard sell, but I told him about the great medicinal value of the honey. He must have fallen sick, but the bastard is still hanging in there. Don't worry. I plan on paying a visit to the hospital to see how my buddy Orwin is doing."

Brighton knew he wasn't his buddy, and she also knew what he was insinuating.

"But why? Why try to hurt these people? They weren't the ones who hurt your mom. Those people are long gone."

"It doesn't matter. My momma never did anything wrong to hurt anyone either. This town was never nice to Momma. She helped people all those years, but she also went through so much grief after losing my sister and father. And everything that happened to her as a kid. And what does she get? Accusations, jeers, and being accused of being a witch. They laughed when she wanted to get her book published. Well, we were going to get the last laugh. Bradertown would feel the true effects of My Skull Possession, and my momma's wish of getting her book out there would be fulfilled. With a little bonus," he said laughing.

Brighton thought about what approach she should take. He seemed to like talking about his mother and stayed pretty calm by saying that. But knowing what his plans were for Orwin, and of course, the fact that Richard showed no remorse over murdering all of those people, she knew her safety was in jeopardy. After everything he just told her, there was no way he was letting her go.

"Don't you think your mom would have been upset knowing you hurt all those people? You said she helped people all her life. She would probably be sad knowing what you did. She would never want people associating her book with something so evil."

Richard stood up and swiped his arm across the table. Bottles smashed against the wall, shards of glass spraying everywhere and sticking in Brighton's hair. The smell of lavender, menthol, and licorice combined to make a robust sickening scent around her.

"She would be proud of me. I couldn't help that my dad and sister got sick. I couldn't protect Momma when everyone in the town turned against her. But I could get revenge, and I could do right by her," he screamed.

His voice quivered as he babbled on about how

it wasn't fair and people had to pay. He lunged forward, and Brighton jumped out of the way. He was caught off balance, his shoulder landing on the table. The remaining jars, bottles, and bags spilled onto the floor, and he landed near her feet with a thud. Brighton fell backward, her head hitting the wall. She looked over and saw Richard trying to get to his knees. Brighton reached down, grabbed one of the jars that was intact, and stashed it in her pocket. She didn't bother looking for her phone, but when her shaking hand was able to undo the lock, she ran as if her life depended on it. And it did.

CHAPTER THIRTY-TWO
SOMETHING WASN'T RIGHT

Brighton stumbled as she jumped off the porch. She felt like she was in a movie, running as fast as she possibly could. Her legs felt numb and her feet pounded against the ground. She knew the banging she heard behind her was the door slamming against the porch. Richard Karen, or Richard Karender as she now knew, was close behind. An unintelligible sound echoed against the trees behind her, but she couldn't turn back to look. Brighton didn't want to turn back to look. At any second, she expected to feel a sharp tug on her jacket, but as she made her way to the dirt road, Brighton continued her pace and hoped she was pulling away from Richard. The road was in sight, and she knew if she could make it to the main road, she would then be able to head to one of the houses. Brighton prayed someone was home or willing to answer the door for a hysterical girl. The footsteps behind her continued, and her lungs burned as she pushed herself to make it to the road. The sound of a car in the distance gave her hope, and Brighton sprinted with everything she had so she could make it to the end of the trail before the vehicle passed her. The car slowed by the end of the drive, and she saw someone sticking their head out of the window. She couldn't believe who she saw.

"Brighton? Are you okay? I called Kate, and she wanted me to check on you," the woman in the car said.

"Peg, unlock the door, unlock the door," Brighton hollered, after slamming her body against the rear of the car. The door was locked, and she could see Richard picking up speed as he trailed close behind.

"Go, go, go!" she said, her foot barely in the door. She lay across the back seat, unable to catch her breath. "Peg, please. Get out of here fast."

Peg put her car into drive and floored the gas pedal as she darted away from the unpaved driveway, rocks and dirt flying from under the tires. Brighton sat up and looked back to see Richard staring at the car, only to turn and run back up the drive. She knew he didn't have a car, but she wanted to put as much distance in between them as possible. She also needed to talk to the police as soon as possible."

"I knew it, I knew it. I called Kate and told her something wasn't right. She explained about Orwin and how he knew that Richard did something that made him sick. I drove right over to the house. It's a good thing you told Kate where it was. It didn't seem like anyone was home, and I didn't think you went there. I sat in my car for a few minutes, and when there was no sign of life, I headed out. Something told me to circle back again."

Brighton realized it was Peg who pulled up next to the house earlier. If she only looked out the window, she may not have been in the situation in which she found herself. Her hand clenched the items in her pocket. She also realized if she left earlier with Peg, she wouldn't have the proof in her pocket either. Peg clamored on about how she knew Richard looked "shifty" when she first met him, and she should have known something was wrong. Brighton didn't pay attention to everything she was saying. Her face pressed against the headrest as she watched the road behind them disappear. It remained empty, with no one pursuing them. When Brighton realized that Richard was not trailing behind them, she turned in her seat and leaned against the door.

"So where to, Miss Brighton? Home first? Police?" Peg said, looking in the rearview mirror.

"Is Kate still at the hospital?" she asked.

"Yes, ma'am. That's where we're headed?"

"Yes, please, Peg. Thank you."

Brighton watched as the trees whisked by as they drove. Peg was racing down the dirt road, a cloud of dust encasing the car as they came to the stop sign. Frank Sinatra crooned "Silver Bells" as Peg's car picked up speed. Brighton closed her eyes and tried not to think about all that just happened. She knew if she did, she wouldn't be able to breathe.

CHAPTER THIRTY-THREE
NO COFFEE OR TEA FOR ME, THANK YOU

Kate sat across from Brighton in the nearly empty hospital waiting area. Brighton wanted to talk to Kate the most, but she was also relieved her mom and the police were at the hospital waiting for her. Her mother, who was usually skeptical about everything, only hugged her daughter when she walked into the room. Brighton knew her mom understood the danger she was in and realized how dire the situation was. She didn't lecture her about the book, saying how she knew it wasn't possessed all along. The situation with Richard was real, and much more dangerous than the thought of a haunted object. The deaths in the town may not have been due to a cursed book, but instead a vengeful and evil individual. Not knowing what would have happened if she didn't get out of Richard's house made her shudder. She understood the strong hug, muffled sobs, and unspoken words from her mom more than anything she could have said.

"So, what did the police say?" Kate asked. Smeared makeup and puffiness marred her ordinarily smooth complexion.

"They had a lot of questions about Richard. Why I went to his house, how we made the connections, things like that. And they, well..." Brighton paused. She didn't want to discuss with Kate the fact that the police had several questions about Kate's dad and his store.

Once she explained how Richard used The Book Cellar as an outlet for the book that was causing all the fear in town, they realized how he manipulated the Dorns, making them seem like they were the only game in town to buy the book. If any foul play was ever suspected, it would be on the new guy, the one that not many people knew much about.

"I know. They had questions about my family and me. I get it. Things really went sideways when we moved to town. Then throw into the mix my history. That would make anyone skeptical," Kate said.

Brighton reached over and squeezed her hand. She didn't want to bring up the fact she was guilty of skepticism at one point, too. Having doubt about Kate and her family was something she regretted.

"The investigator talked to my dad already. Once they realized all of our stories matched, I think they felt pretty comfortable placing their focus on Richard."

A nurse walked over and leaned on the armrest near Brighton. "Can I get you girls some coffee or tea?" she whispered in a sympathetic voice.

Brighton and Kate looked at each other and

laughed. Coffee or tea was the last thing they wanted right now—or possibly ever again. Both immediately shook their heads no.

"How is Orwin?" Brighton asked. She watched as Kate smoothed her pants as she stood up and started walking down the hall.

"Why don't you come and see for yourself? He'll be thrilled to see you."

They walked down the hall, and Brighton smiled as boisterous laughter poured out of the room. As they walked in, two nurses sat wide-eyed as Orwin held court from the hospital bed.

"Ohhhh, and there she is, the heroine of the day," he proclaimed as they walked in. He was sitting up, complete in a black robe. He wore his round glasses, but the hospital stay took its toll on the matching shape of his face.

"I'm far from being a hero, Orwin," Brighton said, walking over to the bed and leaning over to hug him. "Those people died senselessly. If we only found out sooner. And where is Richard now? The police said there was no trace of him when they got to his place."

"Oh stop, my dear. If you never went to his house and found the proof of what he was doing, this could have kept on happening. I'm so glad you are okay," he said, in his usual sing-song voice. It was good to hear his exuberant self again.

Brighton knew he was right. Richard didn't count on being seen that day at The Book Cellar, nor did he know she paid a visit to his house. The fact she made the connection with Clara's name and his tattoo, and that he had the book at his store meant he may have had a deeper relationship to *My Skull Possession*, but she didn't expect to uncover what she did when looking around his house.

"I guess he didn't expect anyone ever to connect him to the book. No one would think to look into the tea or honey as the cause of the poisoning," she said.

"And Richard miscalculated how much tea and honey this little round guy would need to knock me off," he said patting his stomach. "I may have lost a little weight while I was in here, but my large waistband is what saved your portly friend."

"The police confiscated everything from his home and shut down the coffee shop. They are running tests on both the tea and the honey."

"Why was he so angry? And what did any of those victims have to do with his mother?" Kate asked.

Brighton recalled the look on his face when she was sitting at the table in his trailer. That look reflected years of pain and grief. If he hadn't been responsible for all of the poisoning deaths, Brighton could almost feel sorry for him. In his eyes, his mother was wronged and mistreated by those around her. When the blame shifted to her for the death of her daughter and husband, I think that was his breaking point.

"I don't know. He spoke of this crazy revenge plan, after everything his mother went through. The fact that she wanted to get her book published so badly was just another reason to go through with his plan," Brighton said.

Orwin leaned forward in his bed. "Oh please. Do you know how popular *My Skull Possession* will be now? Now that readers know it is safe to read it, they'll want to get their hands on a copy. Kate, make sure you ask your dad if he can give me a few copies. I need those in my store."

The nurse eased him back into bed, explaining that a man who was unconscious for days still needs to take it easy.

"Orwin, please rest. There will be plenty of time to get back to selling at your store," Kate said, leaning in for a hug before they left.

Brighton and Kate made their way toward the exit, where their parents would be waiting for them. A little woman came running toward them swinging her hands. It was Peg.

"Girls, girls, follow me out the back way. There seems to be a slew of television cameras waiting outside for you. I told your parents to head back there too."

Brighton appreciated her persistence. It very well just may be what saved her life today.

Chapter Thirty-Four
Oh, Honey, Don't Brush it Off

It was almost a month since the incident at Richard's house. The tests showed the extremely high concentration of rhododendron in the tea and honey. If someone used both every day, it was toxic enough to be harmful or deadly. Brighton didn't rest well knowing the police could not track him down. She and her mom had a police officer near their home for almost a week, but they figured that coming back to this town was the last thing Richard would do. Still, she couldn't help looking over her shoulder wherever she went and double checking all of the locks in her home. The new security system her mom installed put her mind somewhat at ease. One of the main reasons she was able to get through each day after her experience was she had some very dear friends who understood.

It was cold waiting in the long line. She saw the door to the curiosity shop slowly push open. A short, plump hand waved frantically toward the storefront.

"Brighton, Kate, get in here," Orwin shrieked from the crack in the door. Brighton felt a little guilty walking to the front of the line of those waiting for the store to open. They squeezed through the door and pulled it tightly closed behind them. "Isn't this fabulous? Look at that line out there. And only one week before Christmas!"

"You sure do have a crowd out there, Orwin," Kate said.

He walked over and reached up to plant a kiss right on Kate's forehead.

"And thank you, my dear, for asking your dad to give me the remaining copies of *My Skull Possession*," he exclaimed.

"Believe me, after the last few years, my dad wants to distance himself from anything attached to the supernatural," she said laughing.

Brighton wondered if it was the right time to bring up the subject. The focus was on finding Richard and bringing justice for all the victims in their town. But she never mentioned the one thing Richard said that bothered her.

"Hey, so I never found the right time to talk about this, and I think it's best discussed between the three of us," Brighton said, turning her back to the heads popping up and down trying to get a look into the curiosity shop. "Richard said something to me I can't get out of my mind. He talked about everything Lorna went through as an adult, but he also mentioned everything she went through as a kid. It's just that, well, did either of you read the book?" Brighton asked, staring at Orwin and Kate.

They both looked at each other, waiting for the other to respond.

"I ended up reading it," Kate said.

"I did too," Orwin said.

The three of them looked at each other in complete silence. The sound of the growing crowd reverberated off the walls. Brighton knew they were all thinking the same thing. And she knew both of Orwin's and Kate's experience with supernatural experiences. The words written in *My Skull Possession* were either the result of a very talented fiction writer or the troubled countenance of something that terrorized Lorna as a child. Brighton looked at the stacks of books on the round table sitting in the center of the store. The illuminated glass case lay behind the infamous copies.

Orwin walked over to the table running his hand over the books. "Ms. Brighton, if Lorna was writing of a true experience, I do feel sorry for the woman. And if that were the case, nothing would surprise me," he said, picking up one of the copies.

"Can I interest you in a copy as a remembrance?" he said while shaking a copy of the book in front of Kate and Brighton. They both agreed they would prefer not having the book around.

"Suit yourself," he said, tossing the book back onto the pile. He walked to the front and flung the door open in usual, dramatic Orwin fashion.

"Ladies and gentleman, the Antique and Curiosity Shop is open for your holiday shopping pleasure. We only have so many copies of THE book, but everyone will get a chance to see the very things that almost killed me," he said, grasping his chest.

As the customers filed into the shop, there was a golden glow reflecting on the stacks of *My Skull Possession* on the table. The jars of honey and teas were the latest addition to Orwin's strange collection in his store. Brighton wasn't sure if something could harness supernatural energy, but she didn't plan on taking any keepsakes to find out.

Orwin pushed his way through the sea of customers, delighted in the store's sudden celebrity.

"Brighton. I almost forgot. I have something for you," he said, waving them to the back of the store.

"I've been receiving things daily, things people say have a story attached to it." He held up a letter in one hand and a small rubber duck in the other. "This man said this little yellow toy was responsible for causing his son to be possessed whenever he held it," Orwin said while sneering in disapproval. "I'm sure the kid was just a plain old brat," he said, tossing both letter and duck over his shoulder.

"Anyway, that's not for you, but this is," Orwin said, handing the tissue box sized package to Brighton.

She studied the writing addressed to her on the label, but it didn't look familiar.

"There's no return address," Orwin said, waiting for her to open it.

She carefully pulled back the tape and reached inside to take out an object wrapped in rose-colored tissue paper. She placed it on the counter and gently unfolded the layers.

"What is it?" Kate asked, peering over her arm.

Brighton tried to clear her throat, but her dry mouth made it difficult to form any words. The sparse bristles felt like coarse whiskers as she ran her fingers over the brush. The silver was tarnished, but the etching was unmistakable.

"Is that....?" Orwin whispered. There was no need to finish his sentence, as it was spelled out right in front of them.

Brighton's hand trembled as she traced her finger over the cursive script just above the handle,

ABOUT THE AUTHOR

Lisa Miller lives with her husband and children
in the coal region of Northeast Pennsylvania.
She has worked in broadcast media for over two
decades. Her first novel, *The Running Path*, was
recognized with the 2011 Readers Favorite Award
for mystery. When she is not writing, she divides
her time between family and their charming West
Highland Terrier.